Wil  e
at the Dude Ranch

SHERRY WALRAVEN

outskirts
press

*Many thanks to my grandson, Ezekiel, for his idea
of writing about a Dude Ranch.
Good job, boy.
Love ya*

PROLOGUE

1985

As an eight-year-old boy and his twin sister enter the kitchen to find something to eat, they wondered what they had done wrong this time for their parents to send them to their rooms and miss their dinner. This was a common occurrence, with their parents never giving the kids a good reason. It was becoming to be a thing more often as the older the twins became.

The twins waited until their parents went to bed before leaving their room to enter the kitchen for a snack, because it wasn't good what would happen to them if their parents found where they were. They had tiptoed down the stairs on their way to the kitchen trying not to awaken their grumpy parents.

They often wondered if other kids' parents were this mean, or if this was usual parental behavior. They couldn't tell anyone what happens to them, because the parents have already told them they better not tell or what they would do to them would be twice as bad as the first punishment.

After their parents' tantrums and the punishments, they deliver to the twins, the brother has to take care of his sister until she stops her screaming. They were taking a big chance by coming for food. The twins hoped tonight they were sleeping hard and too tired to move.

Tonight's reason for their punishment was because the sister drew a picture of the family. She was proud of her work and wanted to show it to the parents. When their parents looked at the picture, they began hollering at her making her small face scrunch up with fear in her blue eyes making her cry.

"Why would you draw such a picture? If you can't draw better than that, then you should be whipped, little girl. It doesn't look anything like us, and I'm not that fat," screamed an outraged mother with a smile. She seemed to be enjoying thinking about giving punishment to her little daughter.

The father, who wasn't much better than his wife said, "I agree with your mother. Both of you brats go to your room, and you will miss your dinner. Come on, mother. We need to eat," smiled the evil father.

The twins often wondered how they got the parents they have. They see other kids at the playground at the park, and their parents don't yell at their kids, but they smile as they watched their children play and having fun. The sad children would always get tears in their eyes watching the other parents being so nice.

The twins, with heads hanging down, slowly made their way to their room with tummies growling. This sort of thing happened at least three or more times a week. Sometimes it was something like a drawn picture, and other times, it was something like spilling their milk or making too much noise coming in the door. This made three nights in a row the twins went to their room without dinner.

They were in the kitchen to find food, and just when they found something to eat, the parents walked through the swinging kitchen door and turned on the light. The twins stood frozen as they dropped their food on the counter.

"Well, well, what have we here?" laughed a mean-hearted mother who seemed to be enjoying this way too much. It was like this was the only entertainment they had.

The father gave a witch-related laugh and said, "Yep, it's time for little children to go to the basement."

"No, no, no. Please don't take us down there again," said the sister with huge tears running down her sunken cheeks.

The brother, who was always looking out for his sister, hollered, "Take me and leave her here. It's all my fault."

"You have to stop taking up for your sister. You're twins and twins stick together. Both of you come with us and come NOW!" laughed the elated mother.

"Please don't hurt us again," cried the frightened sister.

They all took the stairs down to the basement, or what the twins called the 'torture chamber'. After reaching the bottom of the squeaky stairs, the parents tied the children's hands behind their back and proceeded to put them in a homemade device to hang their bodies suspended from the ceiling. First, they were both slapped in the face with a razor strap.

When the father got cigarettes out of his pocket, the unhappy kids knew this was going to hurt. It had been done to them many times before.

The twins often talked about running away from home, but they knew they needed to be older to do that, and they couldn't wait until the day they could. They didn't know what else they could do.

The dad lit two cigarettes and gave one to the mother. The parents smiled at their kids while they put cigarette burns all the way up the arms and legs.

The parents started back upstairs for a good night's sleep as they told their children, "Good-bye, we will come get you in the morning."

The brother looked over at his sister, "At least, this time wasn't as bad as before. Try to cheer up. I promise you that one day I will get us out of this insane house."

CHAPTER ONE

2020

The beauteous day was sunny without a cloud in the azure sky as eight jovial ladies departed the Delta flight that had transported them to their vacation. The pilot stuck his head out of the cockpit and told the ladies he was glad they had such a good time on his plane. The pilot's smile was infectious and made all the ladies smile along with him.

It had been a unanimous decision among the cousins, who traveled each year to a different destination, to go to a Dude Ranch. One of the cousins lived in Texas, so she had her husband drop her off at the airport to be there when her cousins landed. Not even one of the cousins had ever been to a dude ranch before, and they could hardly contain their excitement as they, after picking up their luggage, searched for the bus that would take them to their annual vacation.

The girl cousins were all named for a city or a state. Their parents must have had carefree personalities to have named their children such weird names. The boy cousins were not named for a city, but after Confederate Generals. Some of the boy cousins were coming to the ranch too, but they decided to drive and see the country.

The ladies who flew to their destination were: (1) Calhoun, who is called Callie. She was somewhat bossy and planned most of their trips. (2) Houston was the same age as Callie and had good reasoning skills. (3) Olive Branch is called Olive, and she laughs a lot and has a boyfriend named, Bob, who she is right fond of, and he will be coming with the boy cousins to join the others later. (4) Berm's name is really Birmingham, and she is a nurse which makes the other cousins feel safer having a nurse in the bunch. (5) Grand Blanc is called Grandee, and she giggles quite often and is extremely frightened of snakes. (6) Alaska keeps everybody going in the right direction at the right time. (7) Jasperrilla is called Jas, thank goodness. She is sweet and would never do anything bad to anybody unless it's called for when somebody needs protection. (8) and the youngest is Phoenix, who is a good one to have on your side if something bad happens, which last year on their annual trip, something did happen which wasn't good. This trip would be better because of all the people who would be walking around the ranch.

The joyful ladies boarded the bus that had a large horse on the side and found a seat, which wasn't hard being as they were the only ones to board the bright blue bus. Anticipation was high as the goofy ladies wondered what was in store for them this year. They had a few incidents on last year's vacation but had better hopes for this year.

Callie, who seemed to be in deep thought, looked at the others, "I have an idea." The others stared at her, because they never knew what Callie's idea might be. Callie liked to do physical things, and she was extremely adventurous. They would probably do what she wanted, because no matter what they thought of her ideas, they usually ended up having a lot of fun with it.

After they all stopped staring at Callie, Berm spoke, "What idea is it this time? The best I remember from last year's vacation, your idea involved chasing a chicken around a yard in grass that was knee high. We did have fun though. One good thing is that I didn't see a whole bunch of grass around here.

"We would have to chase a horse this year," said Jas with a chuckle. Jas was up for about anything. If she didn't like something, she usually didn't say anything about it. "I have another idea to add to Callie's. When someone asks what we do for a living, we can make up any career we want to. You may call me Dr. Kiki, because I'm going to be a brain surgeon."

"You crazies are funny. I was thinking it would be fun to change our names while we're here. I have always wanted to do that. I would need to keep mine just long enough to check us in, since I made the reservation, and then I'll change mine. Dr. Kiki kind of scares me sometimes. Everyone try not to fall and break your head, because the ones you told that you were a brain surgeon, will expect you to fix her."

"Bambi," hollered Alaska in a clamorous voice. She seemed to like this idea a lot.

"All of you may call me Olivia," smiled Berm. I'm sure my parents wanted to name me that, and they forgot. "You ladies just call me Olivia."

"My mama said I looked like a little Angel when I was born, so you sweet ladies may call me Angel," explained a smiling Grandee. They all thought she was teasing about looking like an angel when she was born.

Jas laughed, "We can call Callie, Queenie, and I'll be Kiki." No one knew quite what to say about that. "Or you could just call me Dr. Kiki."

"If you are Kiki, then I'll be Gigi," Houston like those names, because they sound so exotic.

"I think I would be a pretty good Trixie, and I think Phoenix would be a good Jade, and she could be shady and a little sneaky," laughed Olive as she looked at Phoenix to see if she was going to kill her or not.

Callie glanced at the others as she smiled and said, "You know, don't you, that everybody will think we are a troop of exotic dancers."

"I can't dance any kind of dance," chuckled a happy Houston. "No one better ask me to dance or our cover will be blown all to pieces.

"Well, girls, looks like we better learn to dance a little," Olive couldn't seem to be able to stop laughing. "They may have line dancing here, so we need to be ready. I say we get in there and give it all we got. Just try not to look like a goose when we dance."

"This vacation is going to be a good one," said Phoenix (Jade) as they pulled into the driveway to the Dude Ranch.

CHAPTER TWO

The anticipatory feelings of the eight optimistic women were beyond measure as they exited the vacation bus. Looking at their surroundings made them stare with mouths wide open. It looked like it was a good place to have fun, and they couldn't wait to get this vacation started. This is just what the doctor ordered. Relaxation and fun will be what the ladies needed to get away with fun cousins.

The driver of the bus began handing the euphoric ladies a handout of the week's activities. One would think he had just given them a million dollars instead of a brochure, as the happy ladies all began talking at the same time. The driver shook his head, because he didn't know if he could get their attention or not, but he liked to see people happy and these ladies were definitely happy.

"Ladies give me your attention, please. You will be taken to your bunkhouse so you can settle in. You have forty minutes until supper will be served. There will be a BBQ beside the river. You need to decide if you want to ride a horse or ride the wagon to the location of the food. In forty minutes, meet by the corral. After eating, we will have line dancing in the red barn." He could tell they would love these activities, because they were already laughing and having fun.

"Before going to your bunkhouse, I will introduce the staff to you. If you have anything that you need, feel free to ask anyone here. Our staff will be arriving here any moment now. They are here to help you have a good experience, so use them if you need something," said the smiling bus driver.

What the ladies saw next was a sight to behold. Coming around the corner of the red barn was six of the most handsome cowboys the girls had ever seen. They couldn't wait until supper. They were dressed exactly like they had imagined it. Two of them were leading beautiful horses. The ladies couldn't wait to ride and maybe eat with them at dinner.

"Oh my," said Angel with drool drippling down her chin.

"You can say that again," stated a smiling Bambi.

The bus driver looked at the vacationing ladies and introduced Matthew, Mark, Luke, John, Paul, and Jake. "The ranch hands will help you with the horses and anything else around here. Jake will take you to your bunkhouse while Paul and Matthew carry your luggage."

Matthew was the foreman and Mark was his twin brother. Matthew and Mark grew up in San Antonio and they both smile and laugh quite a bit. Matthew is married and has a new baby. He teaches their guests how to ride a horse, along with his brother, Mark.

Luke is nice but he doesn't smile much and keeps to himself. He likes his job and does it well. He has never been married and seems to like it that way, although all the girls think he is cute as a button. He is also sort of a medic at the ranch in case anyone needs medical attention.

John talks a lot and takes a good deal of teasing from the other ranch hands about his talking. He takes the teasing all in stride and laughs it off. He teaches the guests roping. For fun, he likes to fish with his brother on his time off from the ranch.

Paul is super nice to all but doesn't talk too much. He smiles and laughs with the other ranch hands and does his job well. He is the only one of the men who has been in prison for a year for something he said he didn't do, but he has strong faith and will overcome most that happens.

Last is Jake who is nice to everyone at the ranch. He doesn't talk too much and stays to himself. He and Luke take good care of the horses and are nice to all the guests.

The jubilant women happily follow Jake, Matthew and Paul as

they walked them to their bunkhouse. As the ladies glanced around, they saw several bunkhouses around in a circle just like in a wagon train. They couldn't wait to see inside where they would be sleeping for the next week. They were glad they came because the place looks like it's full of adventures.

As they paraded in the bunkhouse, they were amazed at the size of the room. It had a large bathroom on one side, but what amazed the most was the eight beds in one room. The walls were painted a pale yellow with white spreads that had huge yellow flowers on them. It was unique, and they knew instantly they would love staying here while on vacation.

"I'm excited about the BBQ, but there is no way I will get my butt on top of a horse," said Bambi, who had a look of concern on her frowning face.

Jade looked at a concerned Bambi and stated in a humorous voice, "Anyone who doesn't want to get on a horse, doesn't have to. You can ride in the wagon. I'm all for riding the horse." Jade had a nasty experience last year when a rabbit spooked her horse, and she had surgery, but she and Queenie both got the adventurous gene in the family. They always get back up and do it again.

"I guess I could do that," smiled Bambi. She had forgotten they had a wagon to ride. It might be fun. She was sure there would be a lot of others riding in the wagon, so she wouldn't be the only one.

The lighthearted women had finished their walk and stopped by the corral where others were patiently waiting. One of the cute cowboys was explaining that the other staff members would be with the ones riding the horses, beside them, in front of them, and in back at all times. He also mentioned the horses were super gentle, so they didn't have to worry about a run-a-way. The cowboy assured them they wouldn't be alone with their horses. The only thing Jade was concerned about was a dang ole rabbit showing up.

All the crazy women jumped on their horse except Bambi, who was wearing her high heels again. They watched as Bambi slowly sauntered to the covered wagon in her red high heels almost tripping over rocks. The other cousins didn't have any idea why she was so obsessed with wearing her high heels. They made it to the river without incident and had a delicious meal. The table was filled with BBQ, buns, potato salad, slaw, and several desserts. All the talk around the table was joyous as everyone talked at once.

After the trek back to the corral, they dismounted to walk to the red barn where the line dancing would kick off. Fun was had by all as they danced and danced. The wild ladies didn't want it to stop, but it had to end. They had fun telling everyone their fake names. No one has yet to ask what they did for a living, so Dr. Kiki was safe for now.

At the end of the barn dance, the ladies strolled back to their bunkhouse with hearts light and feet sore. They couldn't wait for the festivities of the next day. It would be fun before going to bed to read the brochure and pick out the activities they wanted to do first. They knew it would be fun whatever they did.

CHAPTER THREE

The exhausted travelers entered their bunkhouse with smiles on their faces, tired feet, and sore behinds. All the soreness was worth the pain, because they had an enormous time at the Dude Ranch. The excited ladies like the idea of the owner to name his ranch simply 'Dude Ranch'. It wasn't too creative, but it was nice. The vacationing ladies were having a grand time no matter what the name of the ranch was.

The chatting was loud as the tired ladies prepared for bed. They were told breakfast would be in the area near the red barn at eight the following morning. They didn't mind the early hour, because they were here for the fun and games, and so far, they had a lot of fun. They couldn't wait until the next day to do some other activities.

"Ok, ladies, we need to look at our brochure and see what we want to do tomorrow," said Queenie in a bossy voice. She kept them all on tract, and that didn't bother any of the others at all. "Let's hear your ideas." They couldn't wait to get started with this wild ride at the ranch.

Olivia spoke up with a huge smile, "See what you think about this idea. The trail ride begins at nine-thirty right after breakfast. It lasts only two hours, so that gives us time for lunch. I'm sure we can ride a horse for two hours. Just think of all the scenery we will see along the way. After lunch is the tubing down the river, and after the horse ride, the cool water on our behinds will feel pretty good. What do you think?" It sounded good in Olivia's mind, and she hoped the others would like the idea too. After all, what was not to like.

Some of the ladies were smiling while the others didn't know what to do. Everyone looked at Bambi, because they knew she would be the one who wouldn't want to get on a horse. Maybe if she left her high heels in the bunkhouse, it would be better for her to take a ride on a large animal.

Bambi noticed the others staring in her direction with eyebrows raised and questioning looks, "Okay. If all of you want it so bad, I'll play along. You need to promise me you will help me get up on that dang ole horse though. It does sound like fun. Forget helping me up on the horse. Maybe I can sweet talk one of the ranch hands into doing it."

Some of the cheerful women hollered 'yipee' at Bambi's declaration. They didn't really think she would go for this idea, but miracles do happen on occasion. It sounded like it was going to be a good day. They hoped she didn't change her mind between now and morning. That had happened before, but they were not going to let her change her mind this time. They were going to see to it that she got on that dang ole horse, even it they had to get her a ladder to help her up.

Kiki whispered in secret to smiling Angel, "Make sure you have your phone with you for picture-taking. I have a feeling we may have some Kodak moments for sure. These ladies always have a bunch of Kodak moments, and they loved every minute of it.

"One more thing we need to remember before we go to sleepy land. We told everyone at dinner tonight our fake names, so from now on, we are not really ourselves. We can't forget to use those names, even if it's just us. We need to get in the habit and call each other the other names too," said a thoughtful Jade.

"Good night, Bambi."
"Good night, Olivia."
"Good night, Angel."
"Good night, Kiki."
"Good night, Queenie."
"Good night, Trixie."
"Good night, Jade."

"Good night, Gigi."

"I may have to keep a cheat sheet in my pocket in case I forget those names. I'm not as young as I used to be. Well, maybe I'm not that old," said Trixie as she laid her head on the soft pillow hoping for sweet dreams.

CHAPTER FOUR

I t was a bright sunny day with no clouds in the sky. The sun touching the trees made the leaves have an iridescent shine making the fun-loving ladies feel jubilant as they walked toward their horses. They couldn't wait to ride the trail with their friends and see the sights along the way. The only way they got Bambi on the horse was to tell her about the handsome ranch hands who would be there to make sure they were safe.

"Wait for a minute before going to the horses. I have something I think you might want to know," said Gigi with a strange look on her face. "I overheard a conversation during breakfast between two of the other guests. They were talking about a rumor of a girl going missing last year here at the ranch. The other one said that she had heard that too, and another lady had gone missing the year before that. Oh yeah, they also said that one of the ranch hands was involved in this. Of course, this could be just a rumor. They didn't seem to have any authentic facts, so we won't need to dwell on this."

"Maybe it's just what she said, and it's just a rumor. We probably always need to have someone with us when we go out. Don't go anywhere alone, just in case. It's better to be safe and not take a chance," said Kiki. The other cousins agreed to travel in groups or a least have one other person with them when they were out and about. That shouldn't be much of a problem. Between the eight of them, there shouldn't be any problems.

Trixie's eyes were beginning to widen at the mention of a possible hostage situation. She had been taken by some unsavory men on their vacation last year and couldn't stand the thoughts of it happening again. The others knew how she felt about that situation and would make sure someone was with her all the time. These ladies took care of each other. They were family and family were supposed to take care of each other.

Queenie noticed Trixie's reaction to the news they heard and went to her and gave her a hug, "Don't worry about it. We will all stay close to each other, and It's also possible the ones telling this had bad information. How does that sound to you, Trixie?"

Trixie thought about it for several minutes and decided she wasn't going to let this bother her while they were having so much fun. That experience was long forgotten, but she didn't want to be too sure of herself, so she would stay with the others for safety. She knew her cousins had the abilities to take care of her. They proved that on last year's vacation.

They went to get their horse from Luke, who was doling out horses to the ones who wanted to go on the trail ride. Luke was giving a demonstration of how to mount their horse and was helping some of the ones who still didn't know how to get on their horse. Maybe Bambi will get her wish after all. She had been eyeing those ranch hands since breakfast. She seemed to be almost to the drooling point.

They watched as Luke helped Bambi on her horse. He gave her a shove making her almost go off the other side. The cousins thought for sure she wouldn't want anything else to do with her horse after that, but she was a good sport about it. At least she caught herself before going off the others side.

"I'm OK," laughed Bambi. "And that, girls, is how it's done." With the mounting done, she was ready to ride.

The others had already gotten on their horse and sat laughing along with Bambi. They were glad she was being such a good sport. At least, she didn't have on her high heels. That would have made it harder to mount, for sure.

After the ride was over, the laughing ladies were elated with such a beautiful ride. No one fell off their horse, and that was a plus, also. They all got off except Bambi. They watched her and decided she was afraid to get off by herself, or was she? Luke noticed and went to help her off. He made her day as she smiled and winked at the others letting them know how happy she was. The other ladies thought, for sure, Bambi would probably want to ride a horse every day of the week they were going to be here at the ranch.

"Gigi, we need to find the ones you heard talking about the girls who were missing and see what else they may know about all this," said Queenie with concern. They didn't want anything to ruin the fun they have been having.

"Okay, we need to look around. I'm sure I will recognize them when I see them. Maybe they will be at lunch. If not, maybe they will go tubing after they eat," said Gigi. They needed to be sure the ones telling the story of missing girls had accurate information. They didn't want to have to be constantly on the lookout for strangers who looked like they were killers.

Kiki had an idea of what they could do after the tubing, "I think we need to go exploring later. I saw an old cabin through the trees that looked abandoned. You never know what might be in there. It probably has nothing to do with the missing girls, but it would be something to do before dinner tonight. We might find some unique treasures of days gone by. That would be so neat to show everybody. Maybe it wouldn't be so bad to take a look at the old cabin."

"I'm in," hollered an excited Jade who was a touch more adventurous than the others, except for Queenie, who was Miss Adventure of the World. They thought she needed a ribbon like Miss America. She always like to do physical activities, and no matter where they were, she was always searching for something adventurous for them to do.

All the others agreed to that plan because they needed to stay active while here. Some were reluctant, but finally decided they would go with the others to search the strange cabin. Why not? They didn't have any other plans. As long as the cabin wasn't about to fall down on them or haunted, they should be okay. They would just have to go and see what the cabin was like and if it was safe to go inside.

One of the ranch hands overheard they ladies talking and walked over to where they were standing, "Ladies, you might not want to go to that cabin, because it has been said that it's haunted, and I wouldn't want you ladies to get hurt. Maybe you could go take your picture at the Old Timey Photo House." After saying this, he got back on his horse and left the open-mouthed women. The ladies didn't know what to think about that except they didn't believe in ghosts and things that went bump in the night, so it should be alright to go to the cabin. They knew there was usually safety in numbers, and there was eight of them. They liked the idea of having their picture all dressed up at the Old Timey Photo House. That would be the next on their agenda.

Queenie spoke up as the ranch hand left, "When have we let a little thing like a haunted house scare us away? We don't believe in ghosts. I say let's keep our original plan. Angel, you can walk by me, since you are somewhat nervous around strange things." Queenie was always open to an adventure, and the others usually followed. Sometimes they didn't have a choice. Queenie just took off, and they felt they needed to follow her so she wouldn't get into more than she could handle. The adventurous cousins liked the idea of the old photo. It might fun to dress up in cowboy gear. Maybe they could have the picture made the next day after eating breakfast. Another plan made.

"Sound good to me," smiled Kiki who would go along with anything the others wanted to do. She thought it might be fun, and she didn't want to miss any of the fun they usually had while on their vacations. Kiki was sure they could have fun out in the middle of the woods with nothing at all around them.

CHAPTER FIVE

The snoopy ladies went through the wooded area toward the house that was supposedly haunted. The trees were not near as tall as what they were used to, but it was nice to see other areas of the United States. They saw the old wood front porch of the small cabin and noticed that boards on the floor were gone and some were leaning appearing to be ready to fall. They would have to be careful, because they sure didn't want to break a leg or an arm. They slowly walked up the squeaky steps toward the door that had seen better days. Gigi put her hand on the door and thought, for sure, it would fall in the floor of the cabin. She pushed gently and it opened with a sound that would make a haunted house happy. Some of the girls had an unusual look on their face at the sound of the squeaky door.

Angel looked at the others and said, "I don't think I will be able to go inside that place. It doesn't look like it's a friendly house. I may wait out here on the rotten porch." After thinking it through, Angel decided she needed to be with the others instead of outside on the porch by herself. She remembered what Queenie had said about never being alone. Stay with someone or a bunch of them, so her mind had been changed, because she sure didn't want to be taken by a mad man or a snake.

"Let's go, ladies. How bad could it be?" said Queenie. The others shook their head in agreement to go inside, except Angel. None of the ladies were too sure about this trip to the cabin.

"I'm sure not going to stand out here in nowhere by myself," cried Angel. She couldn't stand the thoughts of being all alone in this strange place, especially in a place that they were told was haunted. Angel didn't do haunted.

They all agreed to split up in groups of two and search the place. It shouldn't take them very long, because it was such a small cabin. It did make them feel safer to be with a partner. There wasn't even a back door, so if anyone was in here, they would have to come by them to exit the cabin. Inside, the walls didn't look much better than the outside. The wood walls were rotten in places and there were several shelves by a nasty stained sink which they thought would be a kitchen. Being careful of where they stepped would be a necessity now that they were inside the ancient cabin. They knew it was just as old as the rotten front porch.

The quiet in the cabin was somewhat eerie until they heard Olivia holler, "Look here. It's a small door, and it has a handle. It's so cute. Maybe a troll lives behind that door." She was excited at the chance of seeing a troll.

"Open it, Olivia. Let's see what's in there. It might be something important," said an excited Jade who like adventure as much as Queenie did.

"What do you think would be important enough to hide in there? Maybe someone put money in there," said an excited Trixie. "It may be gold. You never know. Look what we found last year while on vacation." They knew the chances of it being gold were slim, but sometimes you never know what you might come upon. Whatever they found behind the cute door they were hoping it was something good. A cute door like that couldn't have anything bad behind it.

Gigi walked over to where the girls found the door. She reached down and pulled on the small handle. It seemed to be stuck on something, but it eventually opened, "Oh. You won't believe this. There is a stairway going down like in a basement." Gigi didn't know if she was game to go down those rustic stairs or not. If the other steps were nearly rotten, then these might be also. They didn't need to have anyone hurt.

Queenie was confused because she didn't see where there could have been a basement in this cabin, "This cabin doesn't have a basement. Someone would have had to dig one under the cabin, and it looks like they didn't want anyone in there and find out about that place." Someone took the time to disguise this door the ladies found.

"Let's get out of here. Whatever it is, it can't be good. I say we go back and find a big flashlight and then go down and take a peek. What do you ladies think?" asked Queenie who has a curiosity to know something about everything. Some of the ladies had looks of disbelief, while the others' eyes were filled with excitement.

"I vote no way," said Angel with a disgusted look on her scared face. If she didn't want to stay on the porch, she sure wouldn't want to go down steps where someone had dug a big hole.

Kiki spoke up, "Come on, girls. We have been through worse than this. It won't hurt anything to take a little look. Besides, it may have been sort of a root-cellar to put jars of food in to keep cooler."

"She's right. Let's do this thing," said Gigi who would usually side with Queenie, and Queenie always sides with Gigi. Those two were crazy, and they didn't care who knew it.

CHAPTER SIX

The giggly women made a trail back to their bunkhouse to see if they could find a big flashlight, so they could explore under the cabin in the trees. When they walked inside the bunkhouse, they noticed their beds had been made and the floors had been moped. They sure didn't have a problem with that, because when on vacation, you don't want to spend any time making beds or cleaning. They didn't think there was anything of importance under the cabin, but you never know. They could check this off the list of things to do while on vacation. Some didn't like it, but most were okay with it all.

Angel was the one who spoke first, "Somebody tell me why we are going to search under a cabin in a big black hole." She had that look on her face that she gets when someone mentions doing something, they have no business doing. They knew it was a risk, but their curiosity always gets the better of them, so they would go.

Queenie patted Angel on the arm and told her, "Honey, there is probably no room for all of us under there anyway, so some of you will need to stay in the cabin and wait for us to come back up. We'll let you know what we find down there. It could be something very interesting. You never know."

"Okay by me," said Angel with a huge smile. She didn't have so much of an adventurous nature like some of the others, and the other ladies didn't blame them because of some of the things that had happened to them in the past. This year while on vacation, there should be fun things happening only.

"Why are we just standing here looking pretty? If we're going to do this insane act, let's get to it, so we can go back and find some cake," stated Bambi with a look of wonder on her face. Bambi had a way of getting everyone started. Most of the time when she gets them all going, she always does it with a mammoth smile on her face. Bambi was happy if she didn't have to do any of the adventurous stuff.

Queenie, Miss Bossy Pants, began to take charge, "Okay, ladies, who has the antique lantern we found? Let's hop to it before we change our minds."

"I've got it," said Trixie with a mammoth smile as she held the lantern in one hand and a small shovel in the other. No one knew where she found a shovel and didn't even know she brought one with her. Eyes were big as they wondered what the story was about the little shovel.

Jade began laughing as she watched Trixie with her shovel in her left hand, "Girl, just what in blue blazes are you going to do with that little shovel? It can't be over four inches long. We are not going to bury someone, are we?" Jade always got a kick out of Trixie and her shenanigans.

Trixie gave one of her best Trixie smiles, which is half sweet and half sneaky, "Well, Sugar, you never know what you might find in a hole in the ground. You ladies will thank me if we need to dig a tunnel to get out from under the house."

No one knew what to say about that weird statement until Gigi, who had stopped laughing, said, "Thank you so much, Trixie, for thinking of all of us. We don't know what we would do without you."

"You're welcome. If a wild animal is under there, you will be even happier I brought my shovel, whether big or little. That way we will have something to kill the wild animals with." Trixie said this with another Trixie smile.

"Let's go. Who wants to go down the rotten steps first," asked Kiki with mischief in her deep blue eyes and sneakiness in her heart.

"Since I'm a nurse I'll stay up here with Angel. Somebody has to fix up you yahoos when you fall down those rotten steps getting to the black hole," exclaimed Olivia. What she said made a great deal of sense, so no one complained. They were glad she was with them.

Queenie hollered out, "I'll go first. Follow me. I'll check out which boards are the ones we don't need to step on, and I'll let you know when to skip a step, so you won't break your leg, or anything else important to your anatomy."

"That's okay with me. I'll be right behind you," smiled an elated Gigi. She had that adventurous family gene also. Nothing wrong with that. A person could have worse genes. There's nothing wrong with adventures.

Bambi spoke in an authoritative voice, "I'll wait here if no one objects." She smiled when no one objected.

Kiki looked over at Bambi to see if she had on her high heels. She honestly had on sneakers. Kiki didn't know she had any of those. She thought all she had were high heels. Kiki was smiling at Bambi's sneakers.

"If you're looking to see if I have on my high heels, I took them off because I knew we would be walking and possibly need to get away fast," explained Bambi. Kiki sat and smiled. At least, Bambi was thinking about what may happen. Good thinking.

Queenie and Gigi slowly made their way down the rickety steps without incident. They turned and saw Jade and Trixie, with her trusty shovel, coming down the stairs to help their cousins. Queenie held the lantern high and rotated it around the small room. They were amazed when they saw another door about four feet high on the right of the larger space. It was covered with a large amount of dirt and a small silver handle. Gigi was amazed and smiled at Queenie like they had just opened a great Christmas present. It didn't take much to thrill these girls.

"Listen, I hear something," said Jade with eyes wide open. Jade wasn't afraid, but cautious. She didn't seem to be afraid of anything, except maybe rabbits.

The others stopped and listened. Something was making a moaning sound, making all the upstairs women take notice. It didn't sound good to the wide-eyed ladies in the dark hole either. They knew it was a possibility it could be an animal, because after all, they were underground. If it was an animal, it couldn't be a very large one, so they thought they would be fine.

Kiki hollered down the stairs, "What is making that noise? Can you see anything? Open that door and find out what it could be."

Queenie slowly opened the trap door. The moment it opened they heard a scream that could have made a Rebel proud. It could have been a wild animal. All the ones in the bottom tried to get up the stairs at the same time. They finally made it up after all the hustle to get up there among the cousins who were down in the bottom.

Trixie smiled and said, "Look who is the only one with a weapon, and you laughed at my shovel?" They made it back up the stairs in record time. They ran out the door where the others had already gone. Trixie didn't think the small shovel would have helped in a crisis, but she felt safer for having it in her possession.

"Thanks for helping us out, ladies," said Jade as she looked at the others who ran out the door leaving them down in the basement to be eaten by a wild animal, or whatever that scream happened to be.

"We're sorry we left you girls, but we knew Trixie had her shovel, so you would be safe," laughed Olivia.

CHAPTER SEVEN

T he lone man ambled toward the rustic cabin where he did his best work. He liked this job at the ranch. All the other ranch hands were nice to him and made him feel right at home. He sure hoped he could stay. The guests had all been nice to him also, and the work was easy and fun. He didn't want the bosses to find out why he went to the cabin in the trees so often. He usually made sure no one would see him walking in this direction, because he knew his friends would ask him why he was going there. Sometimes a man just had to be alone to think things through.

While getting closer to his destination, he heard a horrible scream followed by the sound of excited female voices. They were loud, so he hoped no one else heard them. If that happened, there would be too many questions to answer. He didn't want to be caught when he had only begun to do his dirty work, although he was beginning to think about cooling it for a while and lay low.

He slowly crept to the trees and hid the best he could among them without being seen by the loud women. He heard them talking constantly as they got closer to his hiding place. They seemed to be so busy trying to decide what could have made that awful scream, they missed him completely. That was close. He needed to think of excuses he could tell people if they saw him where he shouldn't be. It paid to be prepared, just in case. With all the people walking around here, it could happen.

He wouldn't be finished with the commitment he made for himself for a while yet. He knew when the time would be right to stop, but he wasn't close yet to do what he had to do. Maybe one of the loud women would make a good target. He would need to watch them for a while to see if they were weak and couldn't get away from him when he took one of them. He would need to watch them to decide that.

He also needed another weak man, but one of the ranch hands were out of the question. There wasn't a wimpy one in the whole bunch. He would have to check out the guests the next time they had an activity at the ranch. There had to be a weak man who came for vacation.

It wasn't enough just killing his mean-hearted parents, he needed more to make it all go away, and he was sure after a few more, he would be satisfied enough. He like hearing the screaming of the women as he doled out the punishment just like his dear old departed mother did, while dear old dad was tied up and made to watch. They would then switch places, and mom would be tied up while dad doled out the punishment. He had been to one of his friends' house, and the situation was entirely different. His parents smiled and made him feel welcomed, and they were nice to their kids.

In his mind, he was doing what needed to be done, so other children wouldn't be tortured like his sister and him was. They would pay over and over for what they did to his sister. He had tried to stop the beating they were giving his sister with a ball bat over nothing really, but he was too late. She was already dead as his father swung the ball bat with a vengeance at him and broke his arm and one of his legs.

Luckily, a neighbor called nine-one-one. His parents looked at him as he laid on the hard ground holding his arm, and then they ran away as fast as they could. He found them later after his wounds were healed, and he got his revenge for his beloved sister as he chocked the life out of their hateful bodies. He knew he should feel bad for what he had done, but he couldn't when his younger sister, who meant everything to him, was lying in a dark damp grave. Him and his sister had to take care of each other for many years and he couldn't stop what he had to do. It was becoming an obsession for him. He would do a few more, and then he would be satisfied and stop doing these horrible things. He thinks his sister wouldn't want him to do these things anyway, but if she were still alive, he wouldn't be doing them.

CHAPTER EIGHT

The bold ladies, on their dream vacation, paraded toward their cozy bunkhouse with mixed feelings jumping around the minds of the confused women. They didn't understand why they heard a scream from underneath the rural cabin. Their vacation last year had some awful moments they had not anticipated, and it was looking like it might be happening again. They didn't know for sure yet, but they were hoping for the best. They knew they could take care of situations, but they didn't want to have to do it.

"What do all of you think about the scream we heard in the cabin?" asked Queenie who was a touch frightened and curious at the same time.

Angel spoke up with fear in her voice, "It could be a wild animal. It *was* a big hole in the ground, you know."

"I bet that was it," said Olivia who was still confused, but a wild animal was better than it being a human.

"I have an idea. We could go back tomorrow afternoon after we are finished with our activities and check that place out. We can construct some sort of weapons just in case," Jade had a good idea, and the others seemed to be on board with it. Sometimes the others thought that Jade may have been in the military at some point. They had never heard that, but she was good with weapons and bad situations. Maybe she was in the CIA and couldn't tell anybody about it.

"Good idea," said Gigi, who felt better now that a plan had been made. She sure wished they didn't have to make a lot of plans on this trip like they did last year. At least now, they had some experience with making plans.

As the ladies were getting closer to their bunkhouse, they met

Luke, who was walking in the direction of the cabin. He still had the same sad-looking expression on his face. He was nice to all the guests, although he wasn't big on long conversations. Someone told them that Luke talked a lot, but they haven't seen that side of him yet. Maybe he came out here to think things over in his mind. Everyone needs some thinking time occasionally.

"Ladies, food's almost ready," said Luke with a half-smile making it look like he was smiling on one side of his mouth.

Kiki looked at Luke with a bright smile, "I have a question for you. Do you know anything about the cabin in the trees?"

Luke responded quickly, "No one stays in that cabin. It's a little run down. Some say it's haunted, and others say there is a tunnel underneath it that outlaws used back in the 1800s to make a quick get-a-way. I don't know all that for a fact. It's just what I have been told by the other ranch hands."

"Thanks, Luke, that's interesting," said a smiling Trixie. It was making some sense now to her. A get-a-way for outlaws was intriguing to her.

Luke glanced at them and with a tip of his hat said, "Good day, ladies. Don't be late for supper. It's smells great."

"Wow," exclaimed Bambi, "That gave us a lot to think about. I've never been in a haunted house before. I really don't believe in them, but it might be fun. Count me in, ladies."

"It sure did," said Angel, who was somewhat afraid of haunted places, and of course, snakes. She could get tears in her eyes just thinking about a snake. The animal they heard could be a snake, but snakes don't talk or scream. Thank goodness.

"Here we are ladies. Home Sweet Home," The girls couldn't decide if Olivia was truly happy about the cabin, or if she was being sarcastic. They didn't care either way. They were just glad to be back from their little adventure walk.

The ladies trudged into their home away from home. There was much talk and laughter as they made themselves presentable for the evening meal, "You don't really think that the cabin in the trees is haunted, do you?" asked Angel with a half grin.

"I have something to tell you. The girl that was sitting by me at breakfast this morning is here alone. She's running away from an abusive husband. I think we need to invite her to eat with us," explained Kiki. "Her name is Charmaine, and she seems sad. We need to make her feel better and maybe have some fun with us."

"Yes, that would be great," said Olivia. They were all soft-hearted but could be more aggressive when needed. All the cousins agreed with a smile to have Charmaine eat with them tonight.

Dinner was entertaining to say the least. The cousins, along with Charmaine, sat at a long table with a couple of men who said they were brothers. The ladies of the table didn't quite know what to say when the talkative one introduced themselves. They sat in complete silence while they listened to their new dinner guests.

"Howdy, pretty ladies, my name is Big Dude, and this is my brother, Little Dude. It's so nice to meet all of you ladies. We didn't know anyone else here, so we thought we could be your friends. We make real good friends. We have a friend back home in Arkansas, but he couldn't come with us because he had the gout, so we will be your new friends. Thanks ladies," said Big Dude, who seemed to be the only one of the brothers who could talk.

Little Dude was still sitting with a sad face and not saying a word. The girls thought he must not be able to talk, or Big Dude never gave him a chance. Either way, they would make their new dinner guests feel welcomed.

"OK. We'll be your friends. I'm sure we will have a good time," smiled Kiki. She noticed some of the others had expressions that were not pleasant like they thought Kiki had lost some of her marbles, and sometimes Kiki herself thinks her marbles are gone too.

"You ladies are so nice. Most of the women we know cuss and spit tobacco better than a man. I didn't see any tobacco stains on your sleeves or anything, so we thought you were classy chicks, didn't we Little Dude?" Big Dude smiled showing all the tobacco stains on his big teeth. Guess he must have been in many spitting contests with the wild women he told them about.

Little Dude grunted, which the ladies thought meant he agreed with his brother. The men left the table with big 'good nights' to the awe-struck ladies.

"Wow. That was an entertaining dinner. I don't think Big Dude stopped talking all through the meal. I guess he had a lot to say," said Jade who was sort of the quiet type sometimes. But when she talked, man did she talk.

The cousins and Charmaine agreed to meet at breakfast the next morning to discuss which activities they would do. The ladies wanted to make sure that Charmaine wasn't left alone too long. They weren't sure the abusive husband wouldn't be trying to find her.

CHAPTER NINE

The ladies awoke to birds singing and sun shining brightly in the cloudless sky. It was going to be a good day. They could just feel it. After dressing for the day, the ladies decided to do the roping and shooting classes. They already knew how to shoot, but it wouldn't hurt to have a little target practice, and the roping had to be fun. They couldn't wait, and Angel was ready with her camera, so they would keep more memories. They usually remembered their memories, but it was good to see those memories in pictures too.

They walked out in the beautiful day and headed to the where the huge breakfast was being served. They found Charmaine and sat down at the long table from the night before. It wasn't more than three minutes when their male dinner companions from last night came straight to their table to eat. Their smiles were bigger than the barn, as they looked at their breakfast buddies already sitting at the table. The ladies didn't think they were too bad, and they wouldn't be mean to anyone unless it was someone trying to hurt one of them.

"Howdy, friends. What're we doing today? You don't care if Little Dude and I tag along, do you?" asked the one called Big Dude.

The ladies didn't mind too much about them joining their group. It might be fun to see what Big Dude said next. They were sure all Little Dude would do would be to grunt, but that was alright too.

"Did you ladies hear what happened last night. They found a woman propped up against a tree, and she was dead, dead, dead. They said she had bruises and cuts and even stab wounds with blood running down the side of her head. The worst of it was the sign that was pinned to her shirt. It said, 'Bye Mommy Dearest'," explained Big Dude.

It almost made the women not want to finish their breakfast, because they all were thinking about the sound of the scream, they heard the day before. What if it was that poor women who screamed? They sure hoped that scream was a wild animal instead of a human, but it was looking like it could have been the dead woman at the tree. Now, the women were somewhat concerned, and a little scared. What if the scream they heard yesterday was this lady, and she was being tortured, bless her heart.

After finishing what they could eat, they left to go to their cabin before it was time to go do the roping and shooting. They would concentrate on the activities of the day and try to forget about the lifeless woman that had been found on the ranch. This was a little worse than last year when they had to deal with some bad men and a snake lady.

"I just thought of something. We saw Luke walking that way when we came back yesterday. What if he did it?" asked Bambi with eyes wide. The others didn't think it was Luke, but Bambi may have a point. What would Luke being doing at the cabin when he was supposed to be teaching the guest western stuff.

"We don't know that for sure. It could have been anybody," said Gigi. She usually could figure things out, and she wanted to be fair. She would have to do some more thinking.

Queenie looked to be in deep thought, "When we return from our activities, let's find us some weapons of some kind and go check out the cabin again?" Queenie loved an adventure, but this wasn't the kind of adventure they all wanted, but if it might help another woman from being tortured, then it was alright.

Bambi shook her head, "It's not our place to investigate this poor woman's murder. Besides, what if the one who killed her is still there?"

"Let's head to the roping and think about it later. We don't need to take Charmaine with us, because she is pregnant and doesn't need to go. We wouldn't want anything bad to happen to her. She may not be as mean as we can be, when needed," said Queenie.

"I agree," said Olivia, who was a nurse. She was usually right about such things, so they trusted her to be right this time.

Angel had something to say, "We know it could be Luke, or not. We need to talk about the other ranch hands too." The others shook their heads meaning that's what they need to do.

"Good idea, Angel. Where do we start? We have the four gospels, Paul, and Jake. Matthew seems to be the one who has got it all together. He's the foreman and has a wife and a new baby. He seems to be a great person. Mark is his brother and seems to be another version of his twin brother, so we can count them out," said Kiki.

"I agree with Kiki about Matthew and Mark. They talk and laugh with all the guests. John also is friendly with all the guest. He smiles and talks a lot with them," Jade said with a big smile. "I noticed that John fishes on his off days. Anybody who likes to fish can't be bad, unless he chops the fish up into tiny pieces, which wasn't very likely."

"I kind of agree, but you know, all the talking and smiling can be a good cover-up. What do you think about Paul and Jake? Paul talks and smiles a lot too, but he's been in prison before and we don't know why. Then we have Jake and Luke both who like to keep to themselves, although they are both nice. I think we are at a stalemate, and for the record, I don't think John is a fish serial killer." explained Gigi.

That's when Olivia spoke, "It may not be any of the ranch hands. Did all of you get a good look at the grunter last night and this morning? Little Dude looks like a criminal to me. It could be him." The women couldn't believe they may have been seated with a serial killer at the same table.

Queenie looked at the others. They were all making some sense, "Let's go do our activities, eat lunch, go find some sort of weapons, and then go to the cabin one last time. How does that sound?"

They all agreed and walked out the door to rope and shoot. They were looking forward to learning how to rope. You never knew when that talent might come in handy. They might lasso them a serial killer.

CHAPTER TEN

After breakfast Charmaine went back to her bunkhouse to rest before going to the activities her new friends decided on. She liked all of them and didn't want to disappoint them if she didn't do well. They told her not to worry, because they had never done roping either. They were so nice to include her in their fun. Maybe being with them and doing these activities will help to get her mind off all her problems. She rubbed her growing stomach and smiled. She didn't want anything to happen to spoil her joy of a little baby. She couldn't wait until the birth of her precious little boy or girl.

Her dad didn't want her to marry Sam, but she thought she was in love, and he was so nice to her before they were married. Later his temper would get the best of him, and he wasn't nice anymore. One day she didn't get his supper done by exactly six o'clock, and he lost his temper and punched her in the face. She didn't go to her parents' house for a month, because she didn't want them to know what he had done to her. She was afraid her dad would beat him up or get his shotgun, and she didn't want her dad to get into trouble and go to jail. Maybe she should have let her dad know. Sam would see what it's like to be punched in the face, and her dad would have done it too.

It began happening more and more. After she realized she was pregnant, she was afraid he would harm the baby when he hit her. Her friend talked her into leaving and going somewhere that he would never guess where she was. That's when she saw an advertisement in a magazine for a Dude Ranch. That's how she got here. She never wanted to go back to him even again. If she went to her parents' house, he would find her. She called her parents often to let them know she was alright, but she never told them where she was staying. She didn't know how all of this would end, but she prayed that it would be a good ending. Her parents wanted her to move in with them, and she would really like to, but she was afraid he would come over and hurt her mom or dad. She sure wouldn't put it past Sam to that very thing.

Maybe one day things would change, and she could go home, at least to her parents' house. They tell her every time she talks to them that she is always welcome there, and one day she will go.

For right now, I'm going to try to not think about all that has happened and enjoy the moment. She will think of the little life inside her and smile and make plans in her head about what she wants to do after the baby is born. She knows the new friends here at the Dude Ranch will help her if she needs it, and she appreciates that more than she can say. Maybe God sent them here for a reason.

CHAPTER ELEVEN

Big Dude couldn't help but think of the nice ladies that let them eat with them. He like the way they held hands and prayed the blessing before the meal. It reminded him of his sweet mama, who always made sure her boys knew the Lord and thanked him for what they had. Those were good memories. Maybe these ladies will let them eat with them at every meal.

Big Dude didn't know what he was going to do about his little brother being so down in the dumps right now. He knew why he was sad, and he didn't blame him, but bringing him to the Dude Ranch was something he thought would get his mind off his problems. Right now, he's still droopy, but they had the whole week ahead of them, so that may change. I promised my daddy before he passed away that I would look after Little Dude, and that was certainly what he was going to do.

They would go with the girls to learn how to rope, and surely that will liven up his brother some, and it should be fun for him also. A little fun didn't hurt anybody.

Big Dude thought it would be a good idea if his brother and him could sort of look after the nice ladies that were good to them while here at the Dude Ranch. Not everywhere has only nice people. He didn't know what made a person do bad things, but he guessed it wasn't his problem.

"Okay, girls. We're here to protect you." He would make sure they were safe and happy.

CHAPTER TWELVE

After the activities of the morning and a tasty lunch, the happy women decided to gather some sort of weapons, and then journey to the rustic cabin in the trees. They had gathered some big thick limbs and a ball bat they found in the restroom of the bunkhouse. Of course, Trixie had her trusty shovel, which wasn't much of a weapon, but they thought it was better than nothing, and it made her feel better when she had it with her. They slowly walked up a small hill to the stand of trees beside the cabin. It didn't appear to have changed any since the last time they were there.

"I'm a little scared, but I'll be fine in a bit. I know we can do this," said Angel with a small smile. Olivia went to Angel and put her arm around her for comfort. Angel's smile got a little brighter. She knew she would be alright. After all, she had all the girls with her.

"We're all scared, Angel, so don't worry. There should be safety in numbers. If we stick together, we should be fine," explained Queenie. "We take care of each other. Remember that from last year's vacation."

They heard a rattling in the bushes beside the house, and panic ran rapid through the group of investigative women. It most likely was a rabbit or another small animal, but they couldn't be sure. It began to sound louder, so that knocked out the small animal theory. Gigi was holding on to Angel before she bolted back to the bunkhouse. Angel must have been thinking that it could be a snake, but the girls knew this was bigger than a snake.

The surprise they saw coming out of the bushes was not what

they had expected. It was an elderly woman who was almost as tall as one of the trees. They had never seen a woman that tall before in their life. She must be around six and half feet tall with wrinkles everywhere you could see skin. She had a cigarette that appeared to be stuck in her upper lip, and an antique cowboy hat that must have belonged to her great grandfather. Her pants were somewhat too short for her long frame, but the most unusual thing about her was she had a rope around her neck with live squirrels and rabbits on it. The cousins were somewhat shocked at that.

After the ladies closed their mouths and got their eyes back to a normal size, Trixie looked at the old lady and smiled, "Hi. My name's Trixie and these are my cousins. We are staying at the Dude Ranch over yonder past that stand of trees."

"What's your name, ma'am?" asked a curious Jade who couldn't imagine anyone hanging small live animals around their neck. Jade was curious, but she began to see the lady was okay the more she looked at her. She looked big, but harmless.

"My name's Tinker," said the old woman without a smile. She wasn't too sure about these women and what they were doing here.

"It's nice to meet you, Tinker. That's an unusual name. How did you come about having it?" asked a happy Kiki who was trying to be nice without giggling. Kiki loved a good adventure, and this one was turning out to be special. She had never seen a woman quiet this tall before and was amazed just looking at her.

"My Paw saw me when I was born and thought I looked like a little Tinker Bell and that's what he named me. It got shortened to Tinker later on when I was just a kid."

After they all gave their names to Tinker, she looked at them and gave them a toothless grin, "Why do all of you have names like a troop of hoochie koochie dancers?"

"I guess we were just blessed," smiled Kiki who could hardly keep the giggles back. She guessed their names were funny.

Bambi glanced at their best new friend and asked, "I hope you don't mind me asking, but what's with the rabbits and squirrels around your neck?" Bambi said what all the others were thinking but didn't know whether to ask her or not.

"I don't want to shoot one of God's helpless critters, so I chased them down and catch them so I can eat'em," answered the lady with animals jumping around on her trying to get away. They thought it would be rude to turn on the video part of their cell phones, but they refrained from hurting her feelings. They thought no one would believe it without a video.

Gigi couldn't help it. She had to turn on the video on her phone. She looked at Angel and put her hand over Angel's mouth to stifle her laughter. She didn't have quite as much will-power with her re-actions as some people. The other cousins could tell by Angel's eyes that she was trying to hold it in, but she's not very good at that.

Trixie spoke with a small giggle, "Maybe we should introduce our new tall friend here to Big Dude." This made Angel want to giggle even more. Gigi pressed her hand harder over Angel's mouth while Angel's eyes were watering from her laughing. She really needed to learn how to hold it in, but she has never been able to.

"I sometimes use traps now instead of chasing them down. It's a little harder for me to run that fast now that I turned eighty-five. I guess that happens when you start getting a little older," said Tinker with her insane explanation. "I best be getting back to my own place. I thought I saw a jackrabbit run in these bushes, but I guess he ran away. Nice to meet all you lovely ladies." It was amazing how Tinker could talk like a normal person while still holding that cigarette in her upper lip. The girls thought that was quite a feat. She was not one the vacationing cousins would likely forget. They were still amazed about that cigarette not falling out of her mouth when she talked. This was indeed a lady to remember.

"We need a plan before we go inside the cabin," said Queenie who was a bit bossy sometimes, but she was right. They did need a plan. They didn't know what was down there, and they needed to be on their guard and think smart. No one wants to buy a pig in a poke.

Gigi spoke up with what she thought, "I think six of us should go down in case there is trouble, and the other two will stay as look-outs in case anyone comes toward the cabin. I think the lookouts should be Angel and Bambi. We will leave the ball bat with them in case of trouble. The rest will take our weapons and go inside the tunnel." Gigi thought that was a pretty good start to a plan.

The others didn't want to be a stick-in-the-mud, so they agreed with Gigi's plan. At least now they had a plan, so they couldn't complain. Bambi grabbed the ball bat quickly and sat down in the rickety straight-backed chair in front of a window to be a lookout. Angel grabbed the other straight-backed chair and turned to sit in front of the other window in the dim-lighted room.

Queenie searched the others' eyes for agreement to get ready to go down under. They were somewhat smiling, so that must mean they were okay with this adventure, "Let's go, ladies, and see what we can find when we go in the dark tunnel. Stay close together because we really don't know what could be down there. Let's try to think positive about all this. We know we thought we saw knives and some other stuff before when we opened the door, but we have more light this time to take a better look."

CHAPTER THIRTEEN

Tinker ambled on to her small cabin thinking about the ladies she met today. They seemed like nice ladies, and they talked to her. Not many people around these parts would have talked to me like that. They all think she's just a crazy old woman, and maybe she is, but she's happy the way she is, and if anyone doesn't like it, then that's their problem. The nice ladies treated her like she was just as good as everyone else. Those ladies have good taste.

She went to the shed where she kept the cages for her catches of the day. It looked like it was about to fall down on the ground, but she hadn't had the time to fix it. She probably needed to fix it before winter, and she would as soon as she sold enough of her squirrels and rabbits to the neighbors, so she could buy a few supplies.

She enjoyed talking to the happy ladies earlier. It's been a while since she had someone to converse with about stuff. Maybe she should invite them over for supper one night. They looked like they didn't get enough to eat, and she could fry them up a plump rabbit and pick some blackberries for a nice pie. If she sees them again, that's what she'll do. She couldn't wait to see them.

She wouldn't want one of the ladies she met today to come to any harm. Women have been taken around here lately. She knew she was safe, because she was stronger than most men, and she would fight them like crazy before letting them take her and kill her. Maybe she should follow the nice ladies and make sure they are not taken. Yep, that's what she'll do.

CHAPTER FOURTEEN

This time when the cousins went down the rotten steps to the hole with the door to the tunnel, they were prepared with big sticks, more lanterns, and Trixie's shovel. At one point, Gigi almost fell through the step, but Queenie caught her. They would need to make sure when they went back up, to skip that step. They didn't need for anyone to get hurt. It could be dangerous to be down here anyway. They didn't need to be hurt, even though Olivia is with them, she couldn't do much down there to help them.

"What do you think about that old lady we encountered when arriving here?" asked Trixie who wouldn't let loose of her shovel. They hoped the plane would let her on with it, because they didn't think she would let loose of it. It should fit in her suitcase though.

"I think she might be up to no good. Who chases poor little animals, and it was weird that she was in the bushes against this cabin? She could be the one who killed that poor woman that was found against the tree. She looked extremely strong, so it would be hard to handle her if she tried to do something to us. You know none of us has our guns with us, because we flew out here on a plane, so we need to be watchful," Jade was always on her toes and looking at everything around them.

"I see the door that must go into the tunnel. I hope we don't hear anything screaming this time, because we need to go in there and see what we can find out," Queenie was adamant they go inside the tunnel. She thought it would be fantastic to see where outlaws escaped the law. They might even find something they had left behind. That would be so cool. This was almost as good as staying in Jesse James' cabin last year when they went to Missouri mountains.

Gigi searched the eyes of the others and wondered which one was going to volunteer to go in the tunnel first. She didn't want it to be her, but she would do it if needed, "Who is going to be our mighty leader and go in the door to the tunnel first?"

Trixie said, "Since my weapon is the smallest, maybe I could go last."

"Let's not dwell on this too long. It's sort of damp down here which is not good for breathing. Remember that Queenie has asthma," explained a happy Jade. "I'll go first since my stick is bigger."

They all agreed as Jade opened the dirty door with the silver handle. It was somewhat hard to open, but she finally pushed it all the way back so they could enter without any trouble. Jade picked up her lantern, and as she entered, she put two fingers against her lips to quiet the others. The rest of the adventurous women followed Jade as she slowly held her lantern up so she could see what might be hiding in there. Two of the others also had a lantern and did the same. With three lanterns they could see much better than when they were down there before.

It wasn't a large tunnel, but it was wide enough for two to go side-by-side. They did have to bend over some for it wasn't too tall of a tunnel. While looking around they saw something shinny. Jade and Kiki walked over to investigate. What they saw was not pleasant to see.

"Wow. Look at that," They were looking at several knives, some ropes, and a ball bat. That was the kind of things the dead woman had been done to her. She had knife wounds, bruises, and what looked like someone had hit her in the head with something similar to a ball bat," Gigi didn't like the looks of those things. "Maybe this is the place the dead lady was before she was killed. We need to do some more thinking about this situation."

"I don't think I want to be in this dank place anymore. Let's go back upstairs, but be careful with the steps," said Nurse Olivia, who really didn't want to have to patch up any of her cousins. She was on vacation from fixing people, and she sure didn't want to have to fix up family, because it wouldn't be good to see them hurt.

They slowly trudged out of the tunnel and closed the dirty door, "Let's see if we can cover our footsteps, so no one will know we were here."

"Good idea, Jade," said Kiki who immediately started pushing dirt over where they had been standing. Covering their footsteps in the dirt was something they had ever done before.

Kiki examined to see if they covered them well enough, "I don't think I want to come down here too often. It's not a happy place." Kiki walked slowly to the rotten steps hoping she or anyone else fell through them.

What they saw after climbing up the rotten stairs was something they were not expecting. There were two men laying on the floor with blood running down the side of their head onto the wood floor. Bambi and Angel were sitting in a rotten chair with long faces and no smiles. They looked like small children who had done something wrong and didn't want a punishment.

"What did you two do?" asked Olivia who walked over to the two bodies to check to see if they were dead or alive. "We're alright. They have a pulse. They may have a bad headache when they wake up, but they should be alright." Olivia was shaking her head in disbelief at what she was seeing after coming from the hole below.

"Alright, Bambi, you go first and tell us what happened and why you hit these men and knocked them out," said Gigi who was smiling a little too much when she looked at the faces of Angel and Bambi. Their look was priceless like little children who knew they were in trouble.

"Well, it was sort of a mistake, I guess. We saw them through the window, and they headed toward the door. When they opened the door and walked in, Angel and I were on each side of the door. I hit one of them over the head with the ball bat and Angel hit the other one with one of these rotten chairs," explained remorseful Bambi.

"Did you not even think that maybe you could have talked to them to see why they were here first before you knocked the devil out of them?" asked Kiki with a huge smile. She couldn't believe this happened again. Last year on vacation Bambi hit a poor man over the head and they were going to bury him, even though he wasn't dead. This time Olivia was around to take their pulse.

"We're sorry, but we didn't know anything else to do," explained Angel. "They could have been bad men who was going to take us down in the basement and beat us up, or they could have stolen our money, or they could have tied us to a tree, or they may have taken a knife and cut off all our hair, but here we are safe and sound, because we took care of the situation." Angel smiled hoping that would sooth the minds of her cousins.

"I guess it's okay since they're not hurt all that bad," said a tired Trixie who was stifling her laughter at Angel's explanation of what could have happened to them.

"Hey, look. One of these men is Luke. We better get out of here quick before they wake up. We don't want him to know it was us that clobbered him," smiled Queenie. "Run, ladies, run fast. We got to get out of here."

"It's almost time for dinner. We need to get back and rinse the dirt off us and find our table. Charmaine, Big and Little Dudes will be looking for us," said Gigi as she was knocking dust off her clothes while chuckling at what Queenie had said. Gigi was glad they weren't still in that tunnel. It turned out not to be too bad, because the men in the living room floor weren't dead.

Jade looked at Kiki, "Where are those crazy boy cousins who should have been here way before now?"

Kiki told her she wasn't going to spend her whole vacation worrying about those grown men, who were perfectly capable of taking care of themselves, although it would be nice to know why they aren't here yet.

CHAPTER FIFTEEN

The goofy male cousins of the girls at the Dude Ranch were traveling by truck so they could see the country along the way. They were brothers to the girls except, Bob, who was Trixie's boyfriend. In the truck was Stonewall, Beauregard, Lee, Forrest, Pickett, Bragg and Bob. They have traveled far but was finally getting closer to the Texas state line.

"After we cross over into Texas, we'll stop for some lunch," said a tired Stonewall, who was ready to stretch his legs after driving so far. He knew they had taken a long time to get to their destination, but they had stopped a lot to see the countryside.

Lee smiled, "That's good, because I could eat a possum about now." Lee ate all the time and a lot of it. The others didn't know where all the food went since Lee was a rather skinny man.

"After we cross the Texas line, how much farther until we arrive at the Dude Ranch where the girls are staying?" asked a curious Bragg. He was getting tired of sitting and was starving. He was afraid that Stonewall would stop and shoot Lee a possum.

"Maybe around three or four more hours we should be around ten more miles to the state line," said Stonewall who was more attentive than the others because he was driving.

After crossing the line, they stopped at a huge truck stop. They noticed it had a Bar-B-Que restaurant inside and that was a good thing. Who didn't like Bar-B-Que? It felt good to walk around and get the kinks out of their tired bodies.

They noticed six men laughing and having a good time entering the Bar-B-Que restaurant. The restaurant looked to be only half full, so there should be enough room for them all.

As the famished cousins were chowing down on ribs and brisket, Forrest noticed the table of six men kept glancing at their table and talking while looking at them. The cousins were glad when the staring men got up and walked out the door. They didn't want trouble with the locals around here, and they sure didn't want to get in jail like they did last year when the crazy girl cousins decided to go to the mountains in Missouri.

After the flavorful meal, they each paid for their meal and went out the heavy glass door. The six men who had been staring at them during their meal were still outside the restaurant. Before they realized what was happening, the unfriendly men had guns in the backs of the cousins demanding they walk with them to the side of the building.

Stonewall had his gun with him, but it was under the seat in his truck. There wasn't much he could do about getting it with a gun in his back, besides one gun wouldn't do them much good, since they all six had a gun in their back.

"Tell us what you want and be done with it. We're not rich people, so if it's money you want, you may be disappointed," Beauregard said. It was the first thing that came to his mind.

"We don't want your money. We will get our money later and lots of it. You are going to help us rustle some cattle, and then you can go on your merry way. We have horses already saddled and an eighteen-wheeler to load the cattle on. The more men we have, the faster the job will be over," said the one with a front tooth missing, and a wide mustache.

"I don't think that will work for us," said Stonewall. The last thing he wanted to do on this trip was steal someone's cattle. They knew they would ride a horse when they got to the Dude Ranch, but that was for fun.

"We don't care what you think. You are getting on one of our horses and herding cattle onto a big truck. We don't have a problem shooting you boys," Apparently this one they called Edward was the ring-leader. "Let's go get us some cattle, then we'll bring you back here to your truck."

"We've got to find a way out of this mess. What do we do, Stone?" whispered a wide-eyed Lee. Since Stone was the oldest, the others looked to him expecting him to know exactly what to do in all kinds of situations.

"I'm thinking on it," whispered Stonewall back with a thoughtful expression. "Maybe when we're on the horses, we can make a run for it."

Lee was thinking this plan over, "But they have guns."

"Yes, they do, but they are pistols. We would have to kick those horses in high gear, so we would be out of their range," explained Bragg.

"Makes sense," said Forrest whose face was showing some doubt. "Don't they hang cattle rustlers?"

"Probably," said Stonewall. "But we won't get caught."

That's when the men with guns came closer and told the cousins to get in their pickup truck. Some of the gun men jumped in the bed of the truck leaving a driver and another one to hold a gun on the cousins in the truck.

Forrest couldn't do anything without telling the others his secret, "I don't want all of you to hate me, but I've never been on a horse before. I would probably get shot or fall off before then. Maybe I could get the horse to walk."

Stone smiled a devious smile, "Don't worry. If I need to, I'll get the reins from your horse and all you need to do is hang on tight."

That comment didn't make Forrest feel much better, but he figured holding on tight and letting Stone do the running was better than being shot.

CHAPTER SIXTEEN

The hungry women came out of the tunnel and got out of there quickly as possible when they saw what Bambi and Angel did to the two men on the wood floor of the cabin in the trees. They prayed the men would be okay, because they sure didn't want a murder charge thrown on them. As they exited the cabin, they began walking fast to get away from there in case the two men woke up. They sure didn't want to get into trouble. Management could kick them off the ranch, and they didn't want that to happen.

The trees didn't give off as much shade as they needed to keep some of the hot sun off those walking threw them. The ladies were beginning to sweat, but they were rather dirty anyway after being underground in a tunnel, so no harm done.

"Why do these things happen to us? Last year was one adventure after another. So far, it's only one, but it's turning out to be quite a wild ride," said Kiki with dirt scattered all over her clothes and a streak of dirt along her left jaw. The girls all glance at Kiki. It wasn't just her face and clothes that had dirt on them, but her hair was sticking up in a odd fashion. They couldn't wait until she saw herself in the mirror.

"Let's not read too much into this. We might be making mountains out of molehills, and it will be nothing bad," Gigi was right. Sometimes the girls think way too much.

They reached their bunkhouse with the brightly colored walls and bedspreads that was looking good about now. They each took their shower and felt much better without all the dirt all over their clothes and faces. The ladies were starving and ready for a great meal. They were so hungry, they hoped they wouldn't make pigs out of themselves, but at this point, they didn't care what anyone else thought.

"I see our table, and Big Dude is the only one sitting there. We must be a little early," said Jade who was the youngest and eats the most. The others were jealous because she never gained a pound and ate like a lumberjack.

Trixie looked around the table, "Where's Little Dude tonight? I don't see Charmaine either. She could be a little sick or tired because of being pregnant. She'll probably come a little later. We'll make sure they save her some food because expectant mothers need their nourishment."

Big Dude smiled at the ladies, and the way they seemed to have such a good relationship with each other. He heard them say they were cousins. He often wished he knew who his cousins were. Little Dude was all he had. He hoped he would feel better and be finished with his walk and return in time to eat with them.

"Little Dude wanted to take a walk. He should be along shortly. What did you lovely ladies do this afternoon? I had to take a nap because I was all tuckered out. What do you want to do tomorrow? Let us know and we'll join you nice ladies. I don't know what's taking Little Dude so long. Do you have any idea why he is not back by now?" asked Big Dude with a smile.

"We haven't decided what exactly we want to do tomorrow. We'll figure it out later. Maybe Little Dude got lost," said a smiling Kiki. "It would be easy to do in a place you had never been before."

After forty-five minutes, the confused girls began to worry about a missing Charmaine. They decided they would stop by her bunkhouse and visit with her to make sure she was alright. They felt better now. They would check on her and then go to bed, so they could begin another day well rested, and they could do another day of activities without worries of being tired.

They finished eating and told Big Dude goodbye and for him to tell Little Dude they missed him tonight. Big Dude smiled to think the nice ladies were being so nice to him and his brother.

"If you ladies can't find Charmaine, let me know and I'll help find her. Sometimes it helps to have a man along to help," Maybe Big Dude wasn't so bad after all. He does talk a lot, has a colorful vocabulary, and was a little dirty, but he means well. The ladies weren't going to be mean to people unless those people were trying to kill them. Then all bets are off if that happened.

After eating, Olivia jumped off her bench and said, "Let's go to Charmaine's bunkhouse. I have a bad feeling that I don't like. We need to see if she is there, and if not, maybe her bunkmates will know where she is. I will feel much better if we see she is there."

When they got to the bunkhouse, they saw a dim light shining in the window. They lightly knocked on the plain wood door. A girl of around twenty-five answered and smiled, "Come in, ladies. How can I help you tonight?" She smiled at her visitors as they entered the room.

"We were looking for Charmaine. She didn't come to dinner tonight, and we were worried. We know she's pregnant and needs her nourishment, so we brought her a plate," explained Queenie as she looked around the large bunkhouse.

When they didn't see her anywhere, they really became concerned, "I don't see her in here. Is she maybe in the restroom?" asked a concerned Gigi.

"That's weird because Charmaine dressed for dinner, said goodbye to us, and walked out the door to go eat dinner," cried an unhappy roommate, who was now concerned about Charmaine too.

"Honey don't cry. It's not your fault," Trixie was near to tears herself. She was a sympathy crier. If you cry, she cries. "We'll look around a bit, and if we don't find her, we'll go back to our bunkhouse and make some sort of plan to try to find her."

"Okay, will you let me know something if you find her or not. She is such a sweet person," said the sad roommate.

The ladies walked outside and saw Big Dude was sitting on a tree stump waiting to see if Charmaine was alright. When he saw their faces, he had his answer. He would go with them to see what they wanted to do next. They might need a strong man like him.

CHAPTER SEVENTEEN

S am Simpson drove faster than usual to get to his destination. The road was rough with a few holes, but he had driven on worse. He had a mission, and that mission was taking his run-a-way wife back home where she belonged. She's having a baby, and if needed, I'll take that baby when she has it and give it away. There was no reason for her to run away. Sure, I had to keep her in line, and I hit her a few times, but a woman needs that every now and then to keep her remembering who the boss is. I really do love her but why did she have to get pregnant. I blame all that on her.

Charmaine is a pretty girl, and she's mine to keep if I want her. She cannot go running away every time I punch her. She said she was afraid I would hurt the baby. I didn't even punch her in her belly. I punch her in the face sometimes. Maybe she never was a good person. My mama always said that you can't make a silk purse out of a cow's ear. Mama is usually right about things.

My daddy used to punch my mama all the time, and she never left. Charmaine will just have to come to her senses. That's the way life is sometimes. My mama sure wants this grandbaby. I don't know what so special about grandkids anyway, but mama has her heart set on it.

"Sam Simpson, if you run that girl off again, I'll disown you, boy," said his irritated mama. "You go find her and bring her back. She can stay with your daddy and me until that little one is born. She will need some help for a day or two."

Sam looked on their credit card bill to see if he could find a clue to where she may have gone. He finally found an amount of money that was paid to a Dude Ranch. That was the only name it had. He went to his cousin, who has the internet, and they looked up where the nearest Dude Ranch would be. It took a while to search because there are about a million of those in Texas.

Finally, they found the nearest one from their house. It was about four hours away, but that is an easy drive. I best take someone with me, because I don't know what I might do when I see her. I love her is why I try to make her better, and she doesn't understand that. This last time was bad, and I may have hit her a little too hard. All she had to do was get the supper done at exactly six every night. It must have been fifteen minutes after six when she finally had it all on the table.

Before they started out, they were going to call to see if she was there. His cousin, Roy, who was going to ride with him, had a brother who worked there. They gave the Dude Ranch a call. Luckily, Roy's brother, Chad, answered the phone. He must work at the front desk. Chad told Sam to give him a minute and he would look on the computer.

"Her name's Charmaine, right?" asked Chad with concern in his voice. He knew how Sam was and worried what he might do. He didn't want to see Charmaine hurt.

"Yep. That's her," answered Sam with a smile.

"We have a Charmaine Thomas registered here," Chad sure hoped he didn't get in trouble, but he worried more about Charmaine. He was going to see which bunkhouse she was in and give her a heads-up what was going on with Sam.

"Charmaine Thomas?" asked the disgruntled husband. "That's her name before we married. Sam disconnected the phone call.

While getting close to four hours, Sam noticed a sign saying it was ten miles to the Dude Ranch, "Look, Roy, we're about here."

"Sam, do you have some sort of a plan to get her back?" asked his cousin who really wasn't into hitting women. If he needed to, he would help her. Sam is family, but he didn't agree with hitting women for any reason. This may be a wild ride getting her back.

CHAPTER EIGHTEEN

Charmaine was excited to see her new friends again at dinner. Sam, her husband didn't allow her to have friends at home. She has one she sees when she goes to buy groceries. They talk and laugh, but she knew Sam might hit her if she had a friend, so she kept it to herself. The ones she has met while here at the ranch are so friendly, and they laugh all the time. She really wanted to be happy and laugh like them.

She took special care with her appearance because it made her feel happy. No one seemed to judge anything she said and did. The new ladies were good to her and made her feel like she was important. She liked that about them, and how they made Big Dude and Little Dude feel like part of their group. Another thing I love about them is always before we eat, one of the ladies says the blessing just like her daddy always did.

Charmaine knew her daddy wouldn't like it one little bit what Sam did to her. He would not tolerate that and would have probably gotten into a fight with him. She didn't want to see her daddy hurt, but she realized that it wouldn't hurt her at all to see Sam get hurt. She had made a tough decision, but when she leaves here, she is not going back to a house where she had been abused almost every day. If it wasn't physical abuse, then he did the verbal abuse. She is going to ask her new friends at dinner tonight if they would help her find somewhere to go.

As Charmaine walked out the bunkhouse door, she saw Chad coming toward her. She knew Chad because he was Sam's cousin. He was nice and didn't seem to have a bad bone in his body. She wondered why he was coming to her bunkhouse. Maybe he just wants to say hello.

"Charmaine, I need to talk to you before you go to dinner to-night," said Chad without a smile.

"Is something wrong, Chad? You seem sad. Are you feeling bad?" asked a concerned Charmaine.

"I feel fine. It's about Sam. He found out where you are, and he's coming here to get you. I know how he treats you, Charmaine, and I am trying to help you. Is there anywhere you can hide?" asked Chad with sincerity in his voice.

Charmaine had tears coming down her cheeks because she was afraid Sam would be so mad, he might hurt the baby. "Yes, Chad. I have made some new friends here who would help me. There are eight of them, so I should be safe with them. I'll go to the dinner table where we all eat together, and they will help. Thank you so much, Chad. I always knew you were a good person." Charmaine hugged him and started toward the dinner area.

While Charmaine walks toward her destination, someone suddenly grabs her by the hair and puts her arms behind her back and ties them with rope. She can't see who her captor is, because he is behind her. All she can think about is her baby. She struggles with him until he turns her around and she sees his eyes through the ski mask he has on.

"YOU!

CHAPTER NINETEEN

s Sam and his cousin, Roy, pulled into the Dude Ranch, Sam noticed bright lights and the smell of food. This was a big place, so he thought he would go inside the registration desk to see which room Charmaine would be staying in. When he walked in, he noticed the shiny log walls finished in a tan color, and the Western decorations on walls and around the room. He sees the registration desk and smiles.

Chad sees him and his brother coming toward him and he cringes the closer Sam got to the desk. He doesn't like men who beat up innocent women, even if it is his cousin. Chad had heard his parents talk about how his Uncle Jeb beats up Sam's mama, so Sam must have seen his dad do that while he was growing up and decided it was the thing to do. Chad was glad he had told Charmaine that Sam was on his way. Maybe she will be in the middle of other people.

"Hey there, Chad. How you tonight?" asked a smiling Sam. "Give me the number of Charmaine's room and I'll get out of your way."

Chad glanced at his brother, Roy, and saw him shake his head no. Chad got the message and would do what he could do to help Charmaine. He didn't see what she saw in Sam. He probably didn't hit her like that when they were dating, so she didn't know what she was getting into.

"I can't give out the guests room numbers. It's against the rules, and I would get fired if I gave it to you. Sorry," said Chad with a half-smile. He liked this job and, and he sure didn't want to lose it.

Sam reached over the registration desk and grabbed Chad with both hands by his shirt collar and shook him vigorously until Roy stepped in to stop Sam.

"Fine, I'll look around and will find her myself," Sam was madder than an old wet hen.

As Sam left the building, Chad picked up the phone to call security and told them the situation, and that it may get out of hand if he finds his wife. Chad was hoping they would find Sam and make him leave.

"Why did you bring him here, Roy?" asked his brother. Chad didn't want to see Charmaine hurt. He knew if he saw Sam do anything to her, he would probably get into a fight with Sam and then he would lose his job. This job had been good to him, and he was happy here.

"I came with him so he wouldn't do something stupid and try to harm Charmaine around all these people," said a fretful Roy. "I don't know what to do. I'll go look for Sam and try to see if I can get him to leave."

"OK but be careful. He's a loose cannon," Chad didn't know what to do. If he can get someone to cover the desk, he'll go help Roy.

CHAPTER TWENTY

The agonizing girl cousins ambled toward their bunkhouse with a quiet Big Dude following close behind. He wanted to help, and they were not going to tell him no. His help might come in handy. This could be nothing but her taking a walk and stopping to talk to people, or it could be someone has abducted their new friend. They sure were hoping it wasn't the last one.

They arrived at the bunkhouse and went in to talk over this situation. Big Dude stood silently in the doorway not knowing if he was invited in or not. He wanted to help if they wanted him. His mama taught him to be nice and help other people in need, but she always said, "B Dude, be respectful."

Trixie noticed Big Dude had not come all the way inside the door, "Come on in. There's a chair over there by the bathroom door. Drag it over where we're sitting and help us plan."

He smiled, "You ladies can call me B Dude. That's what my mama calls me."

The ladies smiled and Olivia said, "B Dude it is. Help us think."

"I would be proud to help, ma'am. What are you nice ladies thinking about this situation?" asked B Dude.

Jade was first to speak, "Maybe she took a walk and wasn't hungry. She could have gotten lost and couldn't find her way back." Jade knew this was a big place, because they had almost gotten lost themselves, so it would be easy to do.

"We need to think who could have been responsible for her absence," stated Gigi. It could be anybody, and that sure didn't narrow it down the suspects. It could be someone who works here or even a guest.

"Gigi's right, let's think," said Queenie with gusto. She gets excited when they start planning. She's a planner on everything, and the others were hoping she would have a good plan for this situation.

"She told us about her husband beating her and punching her in the face. He may have found out she's here and came to get her and take her back with him," said Angel. "He could be here as we speak." Angel didn't want to think about that, but it could happen.

The girls heard a sniffle and noticed B Dude had tears in his eyes. He was trying to hide them, so they pretended not to notice.

"I'm sorry, ladies, but I can't bear the thoughts of a man beating a helpless woman, especially one that was with child," The ladies could tell he was sincere. "When Little Dude gets back, I know he would help us."

"Alright. We have her husband as a suspect. Who else?" said an impatient Jade. She knew there could be more.

"B Dude, we know your brother was on a walk, but would he take a woman. I hate to ask, but he's so quiet," asked Bambi.

B Dude spoke quietly, "I can see why you would say that, but no, he wouldn't. His wife took off two weeks ago and took their baby girl with her. I brought him here to take his mind off his troubles. That's why he is so quiet. He's not usually that way. I'm sure he'll be back soon, and I'm sure he would want to help."

Bambi said, "I'm sorry. He must be devastated."

Kiki gave her opinion on who may have taken her, "It could have been Tinker. I found her to be a little odd. I mean, who in their right mind catches live rabbits and squirrels and puts them around their neck. Yep, I vote for Tinker."

"Kiki's right about that one. I agree with her," said Oliva with a grin. "Put her on the list."

Trixie had an idea, "I would have said Luke, because we have seen him two times at the cabin, but we must remember that Bambi knocked the devil right out of that poor boy today, so he's probably laid out asleep somewhere with a roaring headache about right now."

They all began to laugh at Trixie's diatribe of the story of Luke. Even B Dude was laughing.

"You girls are just too much," said B Dude. My mama would have said you were scrappy and bright-eyed and bushy-tailed. She would have loved you."

"Thank you, B Dude. I'm sure we would have loved your mama, too," said a smiling Olivia.

Kiki looked at the others, "She gave me her cell number. I'll call it."

Kiki punched in Charmaine's number but got no answer. This made them all more worried than ever. They decided to go out and look around to see if they might find her or maybe some signs. It might not help, but at least it was something to make them feel better about not being able to find her.

As soon as they went out the door, they saw Chad, the desk guy, walking toward them. Chad stopped to talk to the ladies, "I'm Chad, and this is my brother, Roy. We know your friends of Charmaine, and we wanted to tell you that Sam, her husband, is here looking for her. Sam is our cousin, and I want you to know we don't condone the way he treats his wife. We are looking for him to stop him from doing something stupid. Do you know where she is?"

"No, she's missing. We're worried sick and are out looking for her," explained Queenie with fear for Charmaine showing in her face.

Before walking away, Chad gazed at the girls and their weapons, "Good girls, I see you have made some make-shift weapons. Sam could use a little attitude adjustment." Take one of these walkie talkies to keep us posted and we'll do the same," said Chad as him and Roy went in the opposite direction as the girls.

The cousins decided not to go to the cabin. It was too dark tonight to take anyone there. They did run into Paul, and they told him the situation with Charmaine and her husband. He told the ladies he had a walkie talkie too and he would help look for them and do what he could to find her.

After searching for what seemed like days, they met up with

Tinker. When they told Tinker what they were doing, she insisted on helping. That kind of knocked out Kiki's idea of Tinker being involved with Charmaine's disappearance. Maybe Tinker has a soft spot in her heart. Looks can really be deceiving.

"I'm going to help. I always take my ball bat with me when I get out at night. You never know when you might run across a bad man. This here ball bat might come in handy. I've used it on more than one bad man," said a helpful Tinker. The girls immediately took Tinker off their list of suspects and decided never to make Tinker mad at them. A ball bat beside the head was not one of their favorite things to even think about.

The women hoped Tinker was the one who found Charmaine's husband. Tinker may be just what that man needs right now. They would continue to search through the night if possible. Off they went with their walkie talkie, all the girl cousins, a man called B Dude, and a huge woman named Tinker Bell with a ball bat.

The troop of searching friends of Charmaine came upon a small chapel, "Look, that little chapel is so cute. It wouldn't hurt to go inside and say a little prayer for Charmaine," said a smiling Trixie.

They all agreed and went inside. Kiki led them in prayer, and after saying, "Amen", B Dude began singing as loud as anyone they had ever heard in church. At least, they thought that was singing. It was more like caterwauling, but his heart was in the right place as he belted out his rendition of *Amazing Grace.* The happy group was now ready to find their friend.

CHAPTER TWENTY-ONE

As the male cousins traveled to their destination of horses and a big truck with their captors, they sat in silence with guns being pointed at them. It didn't set too well with them, but they didn't want to make the gun holders mad. Stonewall, who like to talk to people, had about all the silence he could stand. He thought he would begin talking to them and see what happened.

"Is rustling cattle what you do for a living or is this your side job?" smiled a disgruntled Stonewall. The other cousins sat still wondering if Stonewall was going to be shot or if the crazy men with guns would get mad at him and maybe shoot them all.

"I am a mechanic in a huge dealership here in town. I have a wife and three little kids at home with twins on the way next month. I need more money. She had to quit her job because she's bigger than a huge elephant at the zoo," stated the man in the passenger seat who was pointing a gun at them. Stone was hoping he didn't tell his wife how big she was. Women had a tendency to be somewhat high on their hormones at a time like this, and she was having twins.

"Do you think what you are doing is right? It wouldn't be a good example for your kids," explained Stonewall as he searched the face of the man sitting up front. He thought there might be some hope for this man with all the kids, if the driver didn't talk him out of taking Stone's side.

The driver had about as much as he wanted to hear, "Shut up, Bart. He doesn't need to know your life story. We're going to do this rustling job this one time, get our money, and go back to the real life. If he keeps talking, shoot him."

Bob, who was in the back seat began talking, "My name's Bob and I'm a policeman. There are other ways to earn money besides stealing from people who have worked hard all their lives to get what they have." Bob waited to see if he was going to get in trouble for talking.

"Now it's your turn to shut up, Mr. Policeman, or we will shoot you too." The boss of this cattle stealing hombres didn't seem to have any patience or feelings.

Bart was taking all this in his brain and began to worry, "What do you think the punishment would be if we get caught for rustling cattle? It can't be good."

"Well, they would most likely hang you from the tallest tree in Texas, your eyes would probably pop right out of your head along with your tongue. You will definitely pee all over yourself. All the while your family would be there to see it happen. Your choice," explained Bob, the policeman. "Then your kids will see you do all that stuff, and it will be something they will never forget."

With all the banter about stealing cattle and peeing their pants, they noticed they had arrived at their destination. The prisoners were all looking around at the appealing ranch.

They were sitting in the truck looking at a most beautiful barn they had ever seen that seemed to have been remodeled recently. The pastures had been taken care of and everything was neat.

"Is this your barn? I bet your stealing these horses too?" smiled a thoughtful Stonewall. Maybe if he kept him talking, they could have more time to think what they could do to get away from these rustlers without getting shot.

"Not exactly. I work here seven days a week," said the driver, Pete. "I'm just borrowing the horses."

"Did you ask the owner to borrow them?" asked a curious Beau who wanted to get away from here as much as the others did.

"That's none of your business. Now, shut up," hollered an angry Pete.

CHAPTER TWENTY-TWO

"Why are you doing this? I haven't done anything to you," cried a frightened Charmaine who couldn't seem to be able to hold back tears. She was worried more about her baby than she was herself.

"It's not you, it's all about me. I have my own agenda," explained her captor with a snide smile.

"I deserve to know where you are taking me and why you are taking me at all," Charmaine was giving it all she had to make him let her go, but she didn't think she was doing a very good job. The mind of this crazy person had been made up, and there was no turning back now. She thought if she was let go, then she would tell everyone who had taken her. Oh no! He was going to have to kill her, and that meant her baby would be killed too. That's when she started sobbing loudly.

"Shut up that crying, or I'll give you something to cry about!" Her captor wasn't a very nice person. He looked at her with something in his eyes that said he really didn't want to take her but felt obligated to do it anyway.

All she wanted to do was come here and hide from an abusive husband who seemed to enjoy what he did to her. She always kept the house clean and cooked a nice supper every night. There seemed to be no way to make him happy. His dad always beat on his mother, so he must think that is the way everyone lives. Sam was so nice to her when they were dating, but he turned into a monster at times which resulted in her having to hide bruises. If she stays with him, it's just a matter of time before my baby would be hurt, and she wasn't going to let that happen. She had made the decision to not ever let any man punch her again, so she ran away. Now here she is maybe going to be beat again or worse. She didn't want a life like this.

"What you sitting there thinking about? If it's a plan to get away from me, it won't work. You can't run too fast with all that extra weight you carry in your belly, so get escape right out of your mind, little girl," said the one who was possibly going to kill her and her baby.

"Where are you taking me?" she asked. "I have a right to know."

"You sure do talk a lot. Tomorrow I will take you to a special place I found, and that's where my work begins. It's a decent room under a cabin, but it's too dark to go there tonight. We go in the morning. I'll find somewhere to sleep for tonight. Now shut up." She sure does talk a lot, but she won't for much longer. Her having a baby kind of made him think differently, but he couldn't let that sway his decision of what needed to be done. He had never taken a pregnant woman before and wasn't too sure what to do with this one. He really didn't want to harm a baby.

CHAPTER TWENTY-THREE

The cousins and friends ambled slowly to search for their new pregnant friend who may be in trouble. They were hoping she was tired and sat down somewhere listening to the music coming out of the big red barn. The night was dark and cloudy with not enough light from the moon to help them maneuver through the paths. Some had their cell phone lights on making them somewhat able to move toward their destination. They would try the dining area first and then proceed to the barn where the barn dance would take place.

"If the barn dance has already started, do you ladies care if I do just one dance. I haven't danced in forty years. It wouldn't take me long," smiled an excited Tinker. She thought this might be her last chance to dance to real music. She didn't have a radio or a TV, so she sang to herself. It would be nice to listen to live music. They had to sing a lot better than she did herself.

The cousins smiled at the idea of someone so big and lanky dancing but thought it might be a good experience for them as well as Tinker. They didn't want to take much time, but they wanted Tinker to be happy for a change. They would even hold her ball bat for her. Maybe they could get B Dude to dance with her. That would make her doubly happy.

"I guess we could take the time to let you have a dance in the barn," said an elated Olivia. She like to see people being happy. She saw mostly sad or sick people in her job at the hospital. It would be a good change of pace.

Callie smiled while the others waited for her answer. Sometimes Callie could be a bossy butt, and when she was on a mission, she didn't like to waste time. She surprised them all when she said, "That would be fun. I think we all could dance together with Tinker. One dance can't hurt anything."

B Dude gave his best B Dude smile and looked at the others, "I would be right happy to dance with Tinker if it's a slow dance."

"That's a good idea, B Dude. I'm glad you thought of that," said Queenie with a smile that was as big as Lake Michigan. She couldn't wait to see that. Tinker was around two feet taller than B Dude, but he didn't seem to care if she was or not. "Let's not waste any time, ladies. We have a dance to go to." Queenie was getting excited beyond recognition at the thoughts of a barn dance.

"You girls need to remember that we are only going in there to look for Charmaine's husband," said Trixie as she looked at the others.

"We know, but a little break won't hurt anything. We can look for someone who might be Charmaine's husband while we dance," explained Jade.

They all trotted toward the dining area first which was close to the barn. They all searched the area looking for Charmaine or a person who they thought might be her husband. They looked at Tinker, and she had her game face on. If looks could kill, everyone around them would no longer exist tomorrow. They all knew she didn't like the thoughts of a man beating up a woman, and it made it worse that the woman he beat was with child. The cousins didn't know what Tinker would do if they found him and wasn't sure they wanted to know.

After searching for a while around the tables, they decided that neither Charmaine nor her husband was in the area. They all were somewhat on edge because they couldn't find their targets, but they knew they needed to stay on task and not give up.

"Listen. I hear the music from the barn. Let's go check it out. Charmaine may be there listening to the music. It's worth a try," said Bambi with a large smile.

They all agree and left the dining area to check out the big red barn. The closer they were to the barn, the louder the music became. The barn doors were open, and they could see many people on the dance floor having a grand ole time. Tinker passed all the girls and B Dude and was in front of the line to go inside the barn. She seemed as if she couldn't wait to get on that dance floor.

"Man, she wasn't kidding when she said she wanted to dance," laughed Houston who was enjoying every minute of this adventure. She was anxious to see Tinker dance. She had never seen a woman on the dance floor dancing in brogan boots before. It had to be great. Only one thing would make it better and that was if B Dude got out there and danced with her.

The cousins were not disappointed when Tinker handed over her trusty ball bat to Trixie, so she could go on the dance floor. The rest of the group didn't intend for Tinker to dance alone, so they all went to where Tinker was on the dance floor and started dancing to the loud music. Tinker looked at them like she couldn't believe they would do that for her, and it made her happy. It had been a long time since she had friends. Most people around this area don't want anything to do with Tinker, but the cousins couldn't imagine anyone not liking Tinker.

Jade looked around while dancing for suspicious men who might like to beat women. She saw several suspects, but one stood out more than all the others. He was a big brute of a man with a mean-looking expression on his sour face. He very well could be the one they were looking for, and she wouldn't let him out of her sight while in the barn.

Trixie had been watching Jade staring at a man on the other side of the barn, "Hey, Jade. What are you looking at over there? Do you see someone suspicious?"

Jade pointed out the man to Trixie and Trixie agreed with Jade about him being a possible suspect for Charmaine's husband. They pointed out the man to the others in the group, and they all agreed with their cousins about the strange man who didn't smile. Where they came from, smiling was almost a law.

"Where's my ball bat? I see who you ladies are talking about, and I don't think he is from around here. I know about everybody.

I'll get my bat and have a little talk with him," hollered a mean faced Tinker.

When Tinker retrieved her ball bat and headed toward the evil man is when everything started going crazy in the big red barn dance floor. People were scattering out the back door and ladies were screaming all the way out the door.

CHAPTER TWENTY-FOUR

Charmaine didn't know what this crazy man had in store for her, but she didn't think it could be anything good. She kept thinking about her baby and what she could do if she got out of this insane situation. She knew she couldn't go home or with her parents. Her parents' house would be the first place her maniacal husband would look for her. She wouldn't want to put her parents in danger, because she could never live with herself if she did that.

"Where are you taking me? We have been walking a long way from the ranch," asked a curious Charmaine. It was super dark, and she couldn't see where they might be going until he finally stopped. They could be anywhere.

"Shut up. I'll let you know what you need to know," explained the hateful ranch hand.

Charmaine wondered why her life had to be filled with hateful men. First her husband, and now this unhinged man who was taking her to who knows where. She noticed they were entering a place where it looked to be a place with a lot of trees. She might need to know that later on. Maybe she could pretend to fall asleep, and he will leave for a while. She might have a chance to get away.

"Where are we? Are you going to kill me? Have you done this to women before?" asked Charmaine. She thought maybe if she kept him talking, he would get tired of her and let her go back to the ranch.

"I may kill you to shut you up, but I have another plan. I can't guarantee you will like it, but it has to be done," explained the hateful man who was getting nervous with all her chatter.

"What have I done to you to make you want to harm me and my

baby?" She had to find a way to reason with this insane person. He had to have a soft spot somewhere.

"Are you going to be a good mother. I noticed you're going to have a baby. If I let you live, you will probably be mean to your child and beat them or torture them," the man was almost in tears as he made that last statement. Charmaine was beginning to understand why this man was doing this awful thing.

"No, I will not torture my child. I had a great childhood with loving parents who treated me good. Is this why you are taking me, because your parents didn't treat you very well?" asked a concerned Charmaine. She was hoping she could talk him out of it.

"Maybe. Why do you care? Not all people had parents like you had. Mine beat and tortured my sister and me until we decided to run away. That's when they killed my twin sister. She was my best friend as well as my sister. She should never had been killed," he had tears in his eyes as he related that story.

"That doesn't mean you have to be mean to people. You can be better than your parents. You don't have to do what they did to you and your sister. Please don't kill me and my baby. Give my baby a chance to have a good life," Charmaine didn't know if she could get in his head or not. Probably not. He seemed to be too far gone. They saw a movie like this one time, and it didn't turn out too well. It's hard to get inside a mean person's head if they don't want you to.

He shoved her inside a cave in the trees, "We will stay here tonight, and in the morning, I will take you to my special place," said the tortured boy which was what he looked like at this point. He must let his younger life dwell inside his brain. She didn't think she had much of a chance of changing his mine.

CHAPTER TWENTY-FIVE

Sam searches for what seemed like hours without any luck. He didn't think this place was that big, and he should be able to find her. He had searched the bunkhouse she was supposed to be staying in, but no one was there. He was getting mad at not being able to find her. She was his wife and he could do what he wanted to her. He saw his dad do the same to his mom. He didn't like it at the time, but later learned that was what a man was supposed to do to keep his wife in line. It was true that Charmaine was kind and gentle, but he figured it wouldn't hurt to show her what would happen if she disobeyed him.

He left the bunkhouse and walked toward the area where he could see lights. That's where he ran into Chad and Roy. They looked to be searching for Charmaine too. Maybe they will have some luck, because Chad knows all about this place and where someone could be. It never hurt to have family on your side.

"Chad, why can't I find her. You told me wrong," said an aggravated Sam who was losing patience by the minute.

"I told you what I knew. She may have taken a walk among the property. She will turn up sooner or later. Just what are you going to do if you find her, Sam? You better not beat up on her," said Chad with thoughtful demeanor. He didn't like the thoughts about what Sam may do to her.

Sam searched the eyes of Chad like he wanted to hit him, "You can't tell me what to do with my wife. My dad hit my mom a lot, but they are still together."

"Be reasonable, Sam. She won't be any good for you if you hurt her so bad she can't move, and when you find her, Roy and I are going to protect her from you. She is a sweet young lady and doesn't deserve being your wife, because you don't know how to treat a wife. How would like for someone to do that to you?" Chad may be doing a little bit of good for Sam, because he seemed to be having a small bit of remorse.

"Chad's right, Sam. You're not good for her. She deserves a good homelife without fear. Think about it, Sam. If you don't want to be treated that way, then why would you do it to another human, especially your wife who is a kind and loving person who wants to give her baby a good home," explained Roy, who hoped Sam would listen to them and change.

"Like I said, don't tell me what to do. I'll do what I feel like needs doing," said Sam as he walked away from his cousins.

CHAPTER TWENTY-SIX

The happy group of cousins, the Dudes, and the world's tallest lady called Tinker Bell looked around for what would make all the people in the red barn rush out the back door. What they saw was beyond belief. A large skunk came inside the double barn doors and started sliding across the slick floor on its belly with all four legs sprawled out squirting its stinky juice as it slid along. The happy group backed up beside each side of the doors, where the skunk came in, laughing and couldn't seem to be able to stop. It was hilarious to see all the people run toward the back door trying to all get through the door at one time.

They continued to laugh until Mr. Skunk got his footing and turned around toward the entrance where he came in, making the happy group run as fast as they could to get away from the stinky skunk.

"Wow! That was another wild ride and one I'm sure we won't forget," said a laughing Callie. "Let's go look around some more to the left of the barn to search for Charmaine. We haven't been in that area."

"Has anyone seen my ball bat? I hope we didn't lose it in the freedom run from the critter in the barn," said Tinker as she looked around for her granddaddy's trusty bat.

Angel smiled when she said, "I saw it laying on the floor and I propped it against the outside of the barn so no one would trip on it."

Tinker saw her bat and went to retrieve it, "Thanks, Angel, my daddy gave that bat to me right before he went up to Glory land, so I would have a way to protect myself from mean people when he was gone. We have a few around here, but mostly we don't have much of a problem with them."

"How long has your dad been gone?" asked a curious Bambi.

Tinker put her finger beside her head while she seemed to be thinking about her answer, "Well, I think it's coming on to forty years now, give or take a few years. He was a good ole soul. He was nice to everyone he met except that one time he threw horse poop down old man Earl's well. Daddy didn't take too kindly to Earl making fun of me since I was so tall and all, but my grandpa was tall, so I guess that's where I got it. Earl never spoke to us after that. Other than Earl's well, my daddy was a great man.

"That's a good story. No one should make fun of other people," said Olivia with a smile as she patted Tinker on her arm to comfort her.

B Dude was somewhat sad that he didn't get to slow dance with Tinker. He couldn't dance very well to a fast song. He looked a little like Jed Clampett when he danced fast. He looked at the others, "Would you ladies help me learn to dance to a fast song when we have the time?"

"Sure, we would. Bambi can show you how. She's a pro at that," said a laughing Jade.

"Thank you so much, Bambi. I would appreciate that," said B Dude with eyebrows raised and a big smile. Bambi would get Jade later.

They heard a noise behind them and noticed it was Little Dude. When Kiki looked back, she stepped in a hole and hurt her ankle, "OUCH!" cried Kiki as she began rubbing her ankle. "I'm sorry. I don't want to be a bother."

"Don't be sorry. I'll take a look," said nurse Olivia, who was more than happy to help others. When working in a hospital, you see all kinds of stuff, so she could do most everything.

After Olivia did her examination, she decided it wasn't broken, but Kiki needed to sit for a while before trying to walk on it. That brought the Dude brothers to help. They made a pack saddle with their arms and told the others to lift Kiki and put her on their arms.

They did as they were told grateful it wasn't them who had to ride in the pack saddle.

The helpful men were going to take her back to the bunkhouse, but Kiki said she wanted to stay outside. They took her to one of the long tables in the dining area so she could put her foot up and rest her ankle. She thanked them and told them to go help search for Charmaine, and that she would be alright. She told them she didn't see any boogers out here.

The happy group went to search some more for their target leaving Kiki behind. They knew she would be alright, so they didn't worry about her. They searched and searched and were getting aggravated because they couldn't find her and worried that something bad had happened to her out in the night air. She could be laying in a field somewhere.

CHAPTER TWENTY-SEVEN

Kiki sat thinking about any place that Charmaine could be. If she couldn't go with the others, maybe she could think about what to do next. It was lonely at the tables since everyone else had already eaten their last meal of the day. At least, there were dim lights, so she wasn't completely in the dark. Maybe Charmaine took a walk and got lost, or she could be sitting somewhere when she got tired from carrying all the baby weight around. It was about time for her to deliver.

Another thought came to Kiki while meditating. What if someone took her? She knew that her husband was looking for her and that scared Kiki to think that he may be the one to find her and start beating on her. Kiki couldn't stand the thought of that happening to anyone. Kiki's last thought was that maybe whoever killed the other lady that was found dead by a tree, could have Charmaine. That was the most feared idea she had yet. It made her almost cry to think of that happening to such a sweet person.

Kiki pulled her cell phone out of her jacket pocket and was going to call Callie to tell her the ideas she had thought of, but her phone was dead. That seems to be what happens when you need your phone the most.

She was glad there were others helping in this search. Chad and his brother, Roy, seemed to be good people, and they knew Charmaine. She couldn't see them hurting someone like Charmaine's husband does. Kiki didn't have a clue what made a person do such things to their wife. She knew it wasn't right. Her brothers always teased her growing up, but they didn't beat her.

She sure wished her phone wasn't dead. This would be a good

time to call her son and talk to see how him, his wife, and son were doing. She loved talking to him, because they were always on the same page about things.

Among all her musings, she heard a noise and turned to see one of the ranch hands walking toward her table. He stopped to ask what was wrong, and if he could help. He got to thinking and decided he needed to take this one too, in case the other one decided to have her baby. He sure wouldn't be much help if that situation.

As Kiki smiled at the ranch hand, he withdrew a gun out of the back of his pants and pointed it at Kiki and told her to get up, because she was coming with him. Kiki didn't have a clue of what to do. He had a gun, so she better do what he says.

Kiki got up slowly testing out her ankle. Thank the Lord, it was better, and she was able to walk some on it, so that's when she punched him in the face. Wrong move on her part.

CHAPTER TWENTY-EIGHT

The wretched ranch hand walked behind the guest of the Dude Ranch with a gun pressed against her spine wondering the entire time why this job had to be so hard. He didn't really like hurting people, and he knew he should stop. The past was the past and no one can bring it back and make it better. He blames his horrible parents for what he has become, but he shouldn't, because no one told him to commit these atrocious acts of violence. It's all on him. Nothing that he has done so far would bring back his little sister, who he had loved and protected from his abusive parents for so many years, until that awful night when his dad shot his little sister killing her instantly.

He had to return to the cave where he had left the pregnant woman asleep on the hard ground. He didn't want her to wake up and find him gone. He knew he needed to make an appearance at the festivities of the evening. After all, it was part of his job to help all the visitors have a good time while at the ranch. He liked this job and didn't want to lose it.

He didn't intend to take another woman, but when he noticed this one sitting with her leg up on the bench, he had an idea. The woman he had now may go into labor and he will need another woman to help with that. Hopefully, that won't happen, but you never know. He about lost his temper completely when this lady punched him in the face. That's when he almost pulled the trigger of his gun to shoot the insane lady. After getting his temper under control, he realized he deserved the punch, but she sure could give a good one.

"Don't worry, little lady. We're almost there. You won't feel bad too much longer. In the morning I'm taking you and the pregnant lady to my special place. You will like it down there," said a disgruntled ranch hand.

"So, you have our friend who is pregnant? Where is she? Are you taking me to her? What are you going to do to us? What will you do if she goes into labor? Do you know how to deliver a baby?" asked a talkative Kiki who was trying to get the lowdown on how this was all going to take place. She had never had anything like this happen to her before. Maybe when they arrive at wherever he was taking them, she could think of a good plan to escape. Her mama always told her she was a smart girl, so now is the time to prove her mama right, and she sure didn't want to disappoint her mama.

CHAPTER TWENTY-NINE

The unhappy men who had been traveling to meet with the crazy ladies at the Dude Ranch, sat on haybales in the modern barn whispering about what they needed to do and when to do it. It would take some careful planning since the six men who overtook them have guns and they didn't. Stone had a gun in his truck, and he knew Bob had one on him somewhere. He didn't know where he had it, but he knew it was on his body. Thank goodness, the outlaws who brought them here didn't check to see if they had any weapons. It must be their first time they had done this sort of thing, and that was to the captured men's advantage.

"We need a good plan to get out of this mess. We all have a good mind, so everybody, start thinking of a way out of here," stated an aggravated Stonewall. "First, I think we need to take a walk and look around to see which direction would be best way out of here. We need to run toward a main road. I know there is one, because I was paying attention when we turned down this long driveway to the barn."

"Good, let's go walk around. We can tell them we need to stretch our legs before riding horses to steal some cattle," said a smiling Bragg, who couldn't wait to get back to Stone's truck. Bragg never imagined he would ever have the need to say something about stealing cattle.

Forrest looked at his cousins and Bob and said, "I don't think Bart really wants to do this, but he's only doing it because he needs money for his family. We might get him on our side if we talk to him just right. He would know this country better than us."

"Good idea, Forrest. Maybe we'll see him when we go outside

for our walk. If we do see him, I suggest we talk to him then," said a thoughtful Lee who was hoping Bart would help them.

After walking the grass-free pastures around the barn, they found what they thought would be a good place that looked like it would be the way to get out of this mess they had gotten themselves into. They decided to go back to the barn and talk about what they could do.

"OK, somebody give us an idea," Stone wanted to get a plan made soon before it was too late to make one at all.

"I have an idea," stated Lee. "We could knock out the cattle rustlers, then get in their truck and leave it at the truck stop before getting in Stone's truck. That wouldn't be too much like stealing."

Bob glanced at the others when he said, "It's still stealing, but it would be for a good cause, so we, most likely, wouldn't be put in jail for stealing. I just came on this trip to surprise my girlfriend. I don't think it would be the kind of surprise she would be wanting if she had to get us out of jail."

"Does anybody know how to hotwire a vehicle in case the keys are not in their truck?" asked Forrest who knew he sure didn't know how to hotwire a car.

"I thought of another plan. When we start the process of stealing the cattle, we keep our eyes open for an opportunity to make a run for it. We found the best place to run to, so we are ahead of the game now. When I say go, we would need to go and go fast toward the main road. We need to get off the horses when we get to the road and slap their behinds so maybe they will run back the way we came. That way we won't hang for stealing horses. It will mean we'll need to walk or run back to the truck stop. It's not that far. I paid attention when we were on our way to the barn. What do you boys think?" explained a jubilant Stone.

They all agreed with Stone's plan and wanted to do it as soon as possible. The turned when they heard voices and noticed it was the six rustlers who wanted to bring the traveling men down along right with them.

Beau smiled, "Show time, boys."

CHAPTER THIRTY

The group that was searching for Charmaine were beginning to tire because of the long day and now they had walked what seemed like a year in their search, plus there was the dance they all did with Tinker. They were glad they did that, because it put Tinker in her happy place, that was her Utopia, to have had someone dance with her and be her friends. It made the cousins happy too to see how it made Tinker feel. They couldn't believe they had, at one time, thought she might be involved in Charmaine's disappearance. She wasn't a very good dancer, but she had a lot of fun while doing it, so they were happy because Tinker was happy.

"I wonder if the male cousins of this group are going to make it to the vacation this year," wondered a worried Angel." Last year they didn't spend much time with them, because they had a few problems in the woods and couldn't make it until almost the end of the vacation. Being tied to a tree and spending the night in a house with an abundance of snakes in one of the bedrooms, kind of put a damper on their fun.

They began walking back to where the bunkhouse was located. They thought maybe Charmaine may have taken a walk and was tired and decided to go to her bunkhouse to rest. After all, she was carrying a load inside her. They worried she may not feel good and may be going to labor. Hopefully, there was a doctor on duty if that were to happen.

Callie, who was most observant person in the world, looked at two men who were walking toward them. The closer they got, they noticed it was Chad and Roy. They were glad to see them and find out if they had any luck finding Charmaine.

"Did you boys find Charmaine? We haven't seen the first clue to where she might be," asked a nervous Gigi. It made her extremely nervous to think of the many places and situations Charmaine could be in, and her being pregnant didn't ease her mind any either.

"First of all, we need to tell you that a storm is coming this way, so we all need to go back to the bunkhouses. You will be safe there because they are made extra sturdy in case of storms. We can take up searching early in the morning. How about you ladies meet us in the morning around seven," said a tired Chad. "We did see Sam, and we gave him a piece of our mind on how to treat a wife."

Queenie looked at Chad and was afraid to ask, "Where is Sam now? Is he going to go back home?"

"Unfortunately for Charmaine, no. He said he was going to search for his wife and take her back home with him," that was certainly not the answer Queenie was looking for, but she would try to stay positive about this whole situation. She knew what she would like to do to Sam, but it would be way too horrible.

"We'll go back to the bunkhouse and rest, so we can meet you boys in the morning," Gigi was tired, but would have gone on searching if the storm wasn't coming. She hoped Charmaine wasn't out in the weather.

They watched as Chad and Roy turned to go back to the registration building. Queenie knew it was for the best, but that wouldn't stop her from worrying. The girls all sat around the fireplace in their bunkhouse and prayed for Charmaine's safety.

"OK, ladies, I suggest we go check on Kiki and bring her back with us, so she won't be out in the storm," said bossy Queenie. The others were happy she was being bossy because they didn't think they had the energy to make important decisions, and Queenie loved to make plans.

B Dude had already told the girls that Kiki didn't want to go to the bunkhouse, because she had rather stay outside, and for B Dude to leave her at the dining tables. She thought it was just a little sprang rather than broken. B Dude didn't want to leave her, but she insisted that she would be okay sitting there. He really wanted to go back and check on her. Maybe he would suggest that before the storm came.

Queenie said, "Okay, two of you ladies go back with B Dude to help her walk back to the bunkhouse. Jade and Angel and B Dude should be able to handle getting her back here in one piece."

As Jade, Angel, and B Dude walk toward the dining area, the sky began to darken with no stars or moon to give off much-needed light. The closer they came to the tables, they noticed that no one was there. This really upset B Dude because he is the one who suggested they go. She told them to go that she would be alright and smiled her big pretty smile. The Dude brothers couldn't resist that smile and did what she wanted.

B Dude didn't want to be the one to tell Queenie and the others that their cousin was gone. Her self-assurance scared him sometimes. He didn't know what to do next. The trio turned around and slowly walked back to where Queenie and the other girl were waiting to see Kiki.

CHAPTER THIRTY-ONE

Kiki knew he must be taking her to wherever he has stored Charmaine, and she was praying that Charmaine was alright. The darken sky appeared to be brewing up a storm, and she wasn't fond of storms. She hoped Charmaine wasn't out in the elements where she would get soaking wet. Who knew what was in the mind of a crazy man who like to take women against their will? Kiki knew she needed to think of a way to get her and Charmaine free from this insane man.

"You are walking too slowly. You can try to outwit me all you want, but I will tell you right now. I'm smarter than women and a lot stronger. I have to do this last job, then I will be satisfied that all will be well with me," explained a clueless ranch hand.

"Tell me about yourself," Kiki wanted to get him talking so she could figure out what he was going to do to her and Charmaine. She thought he was the one who had killed the lady they found dead propped against a tree.

"You know all you need to know about me, so shut up," Kiki thought he sounded like he was getting somewhat irritated, but that didn't stop her.

"I get aggravated sometimes with my brothers, but I sure wouldn't kill them. Is that what you did? Did you kill your brother?" asked a curious Kiki.

"I told you to shut up. Don't you listen to anyone? Why would you ask me such a horrible question? I don't have a brother, but I had a twin sister one time," The ranch hand had a look of sorrow on his tired face as he glanced at Kiki.

"Did something happen to your sister?" asked Kiki. She thought she might be getting somewhere now.

"My parents killed my twin sister. Are you happy now? They were evil people who enjoyed abusing my sister and me more times than I can count. We had finally had enough, so we were trying to run away until they caught up with us, and that's when he killed her." The ranch hand hung his head and Kiki thought she heard him sniffling as he cried.

Kiki now knew why he was doing these things to people. He must have been a troubled boy, "I'm sorry. That couldn't have been a good childhood."

"Don't try to analyze me. Just be quiet and let me think," He didn't want anyone knowing his business.

They finally reached their destination. He pushed Kiki inside the cave where he had left her friend. Kiki saw Charmaine immediately as she lay asleep on the hard ground. Kiki came inside quietly so as not to awaken the sleeping mother-to-be. She felt bad this had happened to her friend. He looked around to see if escape would even be possible. If Charmaine woke up, they might have a chance of two against one, even if one of the two was big as a barrel around the middle.

Charmaine began to stir while Kiki was staring at her while she slept. Kiki didn't want anything to happen to her pregnant friend. Charmaine opened her eyes and smiled as she gazed on the face of Kiki. A thousand things were floating around in Charmaine's mind as she wondered why Kiki was there with her. She looked around for the rest of Kiki's cousins, but all she saw was her captor sitting and looking drowsy. That might to their advantage.

"Are you okay, Charmaine? You don't feel like you are going into labor any way soon, do you?" Kiki needed to find out exactly what Charmaine would be able to do to help her get out of this mess. "I sure wish I had my rolling pin."

Charmaine gave Kiki a strange look when she said that about the rolling pin, "Kiki, what would you do with a rolling pin? Make biscuits?"

"I was thinking about what my neighbor's sister did with a rolling pin. It's kind of a funny story, but I wouldn't recommend for anyone to do what her sister did with her rolling pin. Her sister and her husband were both ninety-five years old if they were a day. She didn't like it because he didn't have a job. He just sat outside under the biggest tree he could find in the state of Texas in a straight-backed chair not hitting a lick at work all day. This was what he did every day."

"Then why did she kill him?" Charmaine was intrigued at the story, but she had questions.

"His wife caught wind that he was planning to run away with a younger woman. She was only eighty-two, you see. The wife couldn't understand why he would want her. Every Sunday just as soon as the preacher said the closing prayer, she ran like a cheetah out the door before he got the A out of Amen. Nobody knew why she was always in a hurry."

"The wife couldn't stand it any longer. While she was rolling out the biscuits one morning, she looked at the rolling pin in her hands and got an idea. Out the door she went to the tree where he sat every day and hit him over the head with her rolling pin. As he fell flat on the ground, she noticed that there was flour and pieces of biscuit dough on his head. She said, "Oh well." That's when she drugged him out in the bright sunshine, because she knew he hated to sit in the sun and buried him right there in the back yard in the sun. No one around those parts never knew where ole Bud went to."

Charmaine was laughing, "I'm sorry. I needed a good story to lift the mood some. Thanks Kiki."

"You don't have to worry about me being in labor. I have another month and a half before the baby is due," explained Charmaine with a smile. Kiki knew she couldn't wait to hold that precious baby in her arms, and Kiki also knew she was afraid of her husband and what he might do to her.

"Whew. I'm glad you're not in labor. I don't know anything about birthing babies. I sure wouldn't want to do something wrong if you were in labor. I have had a baby, but I didn't deliver it myself," said Kiki with a wide smile. They both were relieved that her baby wouldn't have to be born in a dark cave at nighttime on a dude ranch.

Kiki whispered to Charmaine, "You try to get some sleep, so you will be rested in the morning. I am going to think of possible scenarios on how to get us away from this insane man who, most likely, wants to do us harm and possibly kill us. Leave it to me."

CHAPTER THIRTY-TWO

Stone kept an eye out for the most opportune time to make their departure from the cattle rustlers. They didn't want to get caught with the other six rustlers, because they had rather keep their record clean. Plus, it just wasn't right to steal, and they didn't want any part of this thing of stealing cattle from anyone. He didn't have a solid plan, but he would know it when he felt it. He didn't tell the other cousins this, because they were depending on him to have a good plan, and when he did it, he was sure it would be good.

The others were getting antsy about the thoughts of stealing. Getting on the horses was making it seem more real to them, and they didn't like it at all. It will be alright, because Stone will have a good plan to get them away from the cattle rustlers before they have to actually steal cattle, or at least, that was what they were hoping.

Stone finally found the opportunity he had been waiting for. He gave a signal to the others of what they had talked about earlier. Forrest, who had never ridden a horse, stayed close to Stone and handed over the reins of his horse to him as he held on to the saddle horn for dear life.

The cousins were riding as fast as their horse would go. Stone didn't think the cattle rustlers even noticed them as they ran away far from where they were. They looked to be too busy rounding up someone else's cattle. The boys didn't know exactly what the cattle rustlers would do to them if they knew they were getting away from them and not doing the job they told them to do, and they didn't want to find out.

The run-a-way men found a place to go in the woods, so they could hide and would have cover. They stopped and dismounted as they slapped their horse on the rump hoping they would know the way back to the barn. They didn't want horse-stealing on their record either, because they hang horse thieves, don't they, or at least they used to way back when.

Pickett looked behind them to see if the rustlers were chasing them. He felt sweet relief when he didn't see any sign of them. He thought going to jail would be better than what the rustlers might do to them. When Pickett turned around, he saw Bart coming up fast behind them. They were relieved when they noticed he dismounted and slapped his horse to go back, also.

Stone walked up to Bart, "If you want to go with us, you are welcomed to come. I was hoping you would change your mind and not go rustle cattle. That's not right. I know of several side jobs you could do to earn more money rather than stealing. That would not be a good example for your children to find out their dad was a thief."

Bart shook Stone's hand, "Thanks, man, for setting me straight. I want my family to think good of me. I don't know what I was thinking before, but I will put my thinking cap on and come up with a much better plan. My parents raised me right, and they would be heartbroken if I had gone through with the rustling plan. I sure wouldn't want to break my mama's heart."

"Good. Come with us. Our plan is to go through the woods and get back to my truck at the truck stop," said a smiling Stone. Bart looked at the others and they were smiling their acceptance.

The trees in these woods were different than the Georgia mountains they were used to. The trees were sparse in these woods making it more visible for someone to see them. They tried to stay out of sight when they could, until they heard a loud sound, they didn't like at all.

"Stone, what was that noise?" asked a nervous Forrest.

Stone answered the best he could, "I don't have any idea, but it can't be good."

Bart, who lived around here spoke, "That, my friends, was a cougar. We need to be on the lookout. Those suckers can jump vertical and horizontal for a long distance."

"What do we do?" asked a curious Bragg, who wasn't too thrilled about what might happen to them.

"Let's try standing behind trees and be completely silent for a bit and see if the cougar gives up and goes on his way," said a hopeful Bart, who was hoping this strategy worked with the cougar.

It wasn't but a few minutes they heard an even worse noise. Bart looked around his tree and noticed that another male cougar was fighting with the other cougar. "Now might be our time to run like the demons were on your tail while they are fighting each other and not paying attention to us anymore."

"You don't have to tell us twice," said a happy Stone. Away they went with the cougars still fighting.

They kept running until they were sure they were far enough away from the fighting cougars, until something grabbed their attention to the right of the wooded area, and it wasn't cougars.

CHAPTER THIRTY-THREE

Sam Simpson search all over what he thought was the ranch area. He didn't think she would wander off the ranch property, but then again, who knows what goes on in the mind of women. He didn't even imagine she would go to a dude ranch, especially when she was pregnant. He would think she would be easy to spot with that huge belly sticking out. The jury was still out on how he felt about her pregnancy. Was he daddy material? Probably not. He would have to give the baby thing a lot more thought.

Maybe he should let her go because he knew she would never leave her baby. His mom was overcome with joy about having a grandchild. He didn't know why she would be, but she was a female and females loved a baby. It wouldn't hurt his feelings if she went to live with her parents and raise the baby there. She turned out pretty good, so they must be good people. He never went there because her parents didn't seem to like him for some reason.

He thought that was a good plan he came up with. He didn't need another mouth to feed, and she didn't like him very much anyway, because she doesn't know how to take a good beating. Of all the traits he could have gotten from his parents, why did he have to take after his father. Maybe women don't like that sort of marriage. Maybe Chad and Roy knew what they were talking about when they told him that it wasn't right to hit her all the time. Maybe his dad was wrong.

She threatened to call the police on him one time, when he hit her in the face and knocked her down with blood running down her face from a broken nose. He didn't want to go to jail. He was too pretty for that.

He thought and thought and came up with the perfect plan. He would divorce her and find him a sturdier woman who wasn't so fragile. She can go anywhere she wants, and he will leave her alone, and she can raise that brat all by herself. That might make her miss him.

If he ever finds her on this dude ranch, he'll tell her his plan. She may cry, because she loves me so much, but she'll get over it. I'll go see if I can find Chad and Roy and tell them his plan.

CHAPTER THIRTY-FOUR

Chad and Roy made it just in time at the registration building as the rain was beginning to pour, and a streak of lightning struck across the sky. They ran inside the building as a boom of thunder came sounding like God was playing a loud drum.

They met Sam on the way back and took him inside with them out of the storm. They didn't know if it was luck or their misfortune to have him with them now. Although they hated what he did to Charmaine, he was family, and they felt obligated to try to talk sense into him about how he treated his wife. Sam didn't like their conversations, but they thought maybe they could help him.

"Sam let's sit and talk this thing out about Charmaine," said Chad with a look of concern on his wet face. "Why do you hit her so much? She's a sweet person who doesn't deserve this."

"I guess because I watched my dad do it to my mom my whole life, and I guess that wasn't a good example for me. It just comes natural to me," explained Sam, who was beginning to look remorseful.

"Would you like for her to do that to you all the time for every little thing?" asked Roy, who was trying to reason with Sam.

"You're right about that. I wouldn't like it," Sam seemed to be coming around somewhat the more they talked about it.

"I have an important question for you that I would like a true answer for. Do you truly love her?" asked Chad with sincerity.

"I don't really know if I love her. I thought she was pretty when we were dating, and I thought she might want to marry me. I supposed I never really just loved her," Sam looked like he was telling the truth.

"You know, don't you, that she didn't sign up for this kind of marriage. No woman would like to be in an abusive marriage. Man, what were you thinking?" Roy looked like he was very agitated with his cousin. "You need to leave her or let her go before you hurt her bad. You know there is a very strong chance that she will not want to go back with you, and I couldn't blame her if she didn't."

Sam turned his back to his cousins like he was thinking, "Of course, she'll will want to come back with ..." That's all Sam could say, because Roy hit him on the head with a board he found on the floor. Sam fell like a sack of potatoes flat on the floor out cold.

"Oh well," said Chad. "I guess he deserved that. Let's drag him down in the basement and lock the door so he can't get away. Does that sound good to you?"

"Let's do it," said Roy with a huge smile. "I've been wanting to do that since I found out what he was doing to Charmaine. She was in my grade in high school, and she was always so nice and treated everyone the same. I can't stand the thoughts of what Sam does to her."

CHAPTER THIRTY-FIVE

As Tinker was putting her catch of the day in their cages, she began thinking about the nice women she had made friends with. They talked to her, and most wouldn't talk to her. Everyone around here thinks she a little touched in the head. She and the good Lord knew she wasn't crazy, and that's all that mattered. She came up with a grand idea. She would cook breakfast for the nice women in the morning.

Tinker began thinking about what to serve her breakfast guests when they came. She didn't get much company and wanted to do it right. Sometimes ole man Greene comes over to eat with her. Tinker thinks he kind of sweet on her, but she didn't want to even think about that. He was okay company, but he didn't carry on a conversation while eating, so she had to sit there watching him gum his meal. The man had no hair or teeth. The lack of hair she could live with, but it was the absence of teeth that bothered her. She never invited him, he just came when he wanted, and she didn't have the heart to turn him away. She didn't think he ever had a home cooked meal.

She went out walking looking for more critters when she saw two of the nice women. She stopped to talk and ask them if they would like to come eat breakfast with her in the morning. They told her they would love to come which made Tinker throw out a huge smile.

Tinker began thinking what she would cook for the ladies she had made friends with a couple days before. She wanted it to be something special. A lot of different things were floating around in her head and she finally decided what her meal would consist of. She couldn't wait for them to come eat. This was so exciting. They had to be better company than ole man Greene sitting at the table gumming his food.

CHAPTER THIRTY-SIX

The girl cousins had a good night's sleep and was feeling good on this sunny morning. They didn't realize they were as tired as they were, but all's well now. They decided to go to the breakfast table at the ranch and tell the Dudes where they would be and would get in touch with them later. They told the Dudes to think of a plan to search for the missing women.

They were somewhat apprehensive about going to eat at Tinker's, but they didn't want to hurt her feelings. She was able and willing to help them find Charmaine and Kiki. They remembered how much excitement Tinker had while dancing in the barn until the dreadful skunk came in and caused a catastrophic event at the barn dance. It was funny watching all the people on the dance floor run out the back door as they slipped and slid on the slick dance floor. The cousins loved a good laugh, and that was definitely a laughable moment.

Queenie looked at the others and said, "I see Chad and Roy. I'm going to speak to them a minute. Gigi, want to come with me."

"Sure," smiled Gigi, who was still smiling about the skunk incident.

"Hey boys, how are you this morning? I have a question for you. Do you think we need to call the police to come help us find the girls?" asked Queenie with a smile. It sounded like a good idea to her, but Chad wasn't smiling.

Chad looked at Queenie and Gigi standing there waiting for his answer, "The hotel manager doesn't want to call the police, because it would be bad press for the Dude Ranch."

Gigi didn't like that answer no more than Queenie did, but she gave her opinion, "Alright, we don't need them. We will find them ourselves. We would appreciate it if you boys would help us when you can."

"Sure will. Keep us posted. I will give the walkie talkie back to you, so you can let us know how it's going. I hope you find them soon." said Chad, who really wanted to help them, but his manager wouldn't like it if he left the desk all day. Maybe when he got off work, he and Roy would join the nice ladies.

"That's okay, we understand. Have a good day," smiled Queenie. She wouldn't want Chad to lose his job because of them.

Queenie and Gigi went back to where they left the others. They told them about Chad and Roy would able to help when Chad got off work. There were the Dudes who were going to help them, also. The felt confident with them, the Dudes, and later Chad and Roy, they would have a good chance of finding Charmaine and Kiki.

They sat a moment and talked to the Dudes to tell them they would see them later when they finished their breakfast at Tinker's cabin.

CHAPTER THIRTY-SEVEN

T he ladies walked the way Tinker told them to, so they could arrive at her cabin for their breakfast. The grass was wet from the storm and some limbs had fallen the night before. The girls wondered what Tinker would make them, but they decided no matter what it was, they would eat it so as not to hurt her feelings. They realized Tinker may not have many friends, if any, so they would be her friend. She lives a sheltered life with her animals and her ball bat.

They traveled on until they saw a cabin in the distance. "Look everybody, I see a cabin and it's in the direction she told us to go. I'm excited to see her cabin. I like rustic cabins." Either Angel was excited about the cabin and Tinker, or she was very hungry.

The closer they got, the more they could see of the cabin. It appeared to be about to fall over on the hard ground. It didn't bother them, because they had seen worse. They would eat and have a good time with Tinker. She has probably gone to a lot of trouble to have them over for breakfast.

As they entered Tinker's yard, they noticed chickens and pigs coming out from under the front porch. The happy animals ran straight toward the cousins. The pigs began running toward Angel which made her begin to run, also. It was rather comical to watch Angel running away from the pigs as they ran around and around the cabin. Her cousins mean well, but they couldn't contain their laughter as Angel ran around the house while being chased by a couple of small pigs and short chickens.

Their laughter was all in fun until they saw a cow with a big milk bag run toward Olivia. She didn't like that too much when the cow started chasing her, until Olivia thought she would run inside the open barn door. Again, the cousins couldn't contain their laughter. Some were bent over double as they watched what they thought would be a good video to send to *America's Funniest Videos*. What Angel and Olivia didn't know was Bambi was filming every bit of this fiasco, and she would be sure to show the others what she filmed before going to bed that night.

The girls glanced in the barn and saw Olivia had climbed a ladder to the loft and was sitting on a hay bale, "Hi, girls, do you like my new home? Get that dang ole cow and cook her for supper. I'm ready to come down."

Tinker walked out on the front porch and threw a baseball at the pigs hitting one of them on the snout. The pigs gave up and ran back under the front porch, and the chickens followed the pigs. After throwing the baseball, Tinker went to the barn and got Olivia out of the hay loft and put the cow in a stall.

"Come on in, ladies. Breakfast is ready," said Tinker with a smile. Tinker was beyond excited.

Tinker's breakfast could only be described as atypical to say the least. Everything was going great with the meal, until the cousins found out what they were really eating. As it turns out they were eating squirrel livers with gravy made from the grease from frying the livers. The scrambled eggs were quail eggs, but all in all, the biscuits were delicious.

They didn't want to hurt Tinker's feelings, but to be truthful, it wasn't bad. Tinker sat with a huge smile on her face at her company. She still couldn't believe she was entertaining friends.

"Wow! Tinker. That was delicious, especially the biscuits. I wish I could make biscuits that fluffy," said a thankful Gigi, who was telling the truth about the biscuits. She didn't have words to describe the rest of the meal.

"Do you have much company? I'm sure you must have a beau coming around," said Olivia with sincerity.

Tinker's face was becoming a little red. Who would have thought that Tinker would blush, "Well, there is one man who keeps coming over to get a free meal, but he's not boyfriend material. He has no hair and no teeth. The hair is not a problem, but have you ever watched a man sit quietly gumming his food through the whole meal?"

The ladies didn't know exactly know what to say to that, and they were trying to keep from laughing at the very thought of a man sitting at this table gumming his food, "We noticed you have some beautiful peonies by the front porch. What do you do to make them so healthy looking?" asked Angel who had a good look at the porch when the pigs came out to chase her around the cabin.

"You may not believe why they are so pretty, but I'll tell you. My neighbor is a good ole Southern Baptist Christian lady. Her name is Margo and she sneaks into the Catholic Church and steals some of the Holy Water to put on her peonies, and she gives me some because she knows I love my peonies," explained Tinker. "She says it can't hurt anything if you are watering God's pretty flowers." The laughing cousins really didn't know what to say about this revelation either, so they just sat silently with tears running down the cheeks from laughing so hard.

"Thank you so much, Tinker. Let us do the dishes since you cooked this delicious meal," said a Queenie with a huge smile.

"I wouldn't hear of it. You are my company, and I don't get company too often. I will not let you do the dishes, but you are so sweet to want to wash them. I have my own dishwasher," explained Tinker. The girls looked around the kitchen and didn't see anything that resembled a dishwasher, but they didn't think Tinker was telling a lie about having one.

Tinker looked at her guests with a smile and sweetly told her company to set their plates on the floor behind their chair. The girls were somewhat confused, but they didn't say anything about Tinker's unusual request.

After setting their plates on the floor at the location Tinker told them is when she let out a huge whistle out of her mouth. The girls were really confused by this turn of events, until they saw a mammoth dog come out of the bedroom and watched as he began licking the plates clean.

"That's a big one, Tinker. What kind is it?" asked Bambi. The others were a little afraid of the dog. They thought after he finished cleaning the plates, they weren't too sure he wouldn't eat them next.

"He's a Bullmastiff, and a sweet dog," explained a smiling Tinker. She was happy that the ladies were interested in her little dog. All the girls could manage was to look at the dog right in the face, which was the meanest looking dog they had ever seen.

"Oh my, Tinker. What's his name?" asked Trixie who was trying to keep a straight face at Tinker's odd dishwashing method.

"I'm sorry. I guess I forgot the tell you. I named him Susie. Isn't that a sweet name for such a good dog?" Tinker was overjoyed they were interested in her precious dog. Precious sure wasn't the word they would have thought of to describe the massive dog standing before them.

With the dishes having already been washed, they told Tinker they had to go. Tinker wanted them to stay, but they told her they had to make another plan to find their friend and cousin.

"Okay. Thank you, ladies so much for coming to eat with me. I love having company," said a grateful Tinker. They all smiled and gave Tinker a good ole Southern girl hug.

As the cousins walked away from Tinker's cabin, Jade said, "No wonder the poor dog looked so mean with a name like Susie. He certainly did not look like a Susie. He was huge.

CHAPTER THIRTY-EIGHT

The male cousins looked at the four men who were holding them at gunpoint. They were a curious looking group. It was clear they were brothers, because of a few similar traits. One of them was extra skinny looking like the other three pushed him away from the table, since they had a sizable girth. The one with overalls didn't have a shirt underneath, and the side buttons had not been buttoned showing that he didn't have on under ware either. The shortest one laughed at everything that was said or done. The men being held at gunpoint thought the tallest one appeared to be the boss.

The old hound dog lying beside them asleep must be their watchdog. Overall Man kicked their watchdog trying to wake him from his nap, but the dog opened one eye and went back to sleep.

"Where you boys heading? Not many people come around these parts. You not up to no good, are you?" said the one who seemed to be the boss. The curious men didn't know if the other three could talk or not.

"We are heading to our truck at the truck stop. Are we headed the right way?" asked Forrest.

"I would say you are exactly where you need to be," again the boss spoke with a gruff voice. The men held at gunpoint knew this one was the one to be nice to. He appeared to have a quick temper.

"Okay, we'll be on our way. Thanks for the directions. We'll let you get back to your business now," said Bragg with a smile. He thought that would be it, and they could get on their merry way. He wanted to get to where they were supposed to be and out of these woods.

"You boys are not going anywhere. You are where you should be," the boss spoke again.

"What do you want with us?" asked an aggravated Lee.

"We figured you could help us build our shed. It shouldn't take long with you all working together on it," said the boss with excitement in his voice. They were all thinking that the brothers didn't know how to build a shed.

Beau said, "We're not builders. You will need to find someone else to help you, and, we will be on our way. Nice to meet you boys."

"You are builders now," explained the angry boss as he stomped over to where the cousins were standing. The cousins knew they needed to think of some way to get out of this weird situation.

The boss seemed to not know what to do next until he stopped and thought for a few minutes. The other three didn't seem to be able to think too much. They stood there and waited for their brother to finish his pondering.

"This is what we going to do. Since it's getting late in the afternoon, we will wait until morning to begin the building. We can start on the shed then. We will take you boys to the barn for the night. Of course, you will be tied up," said angry boss. They wondered if he was ever happy.

The disgruntled men slowly shuffled to the big barn that would be their Holiday Inn for the night. They searched their surroundings to see if there might be a way they could escape these crazy men. All they saw was a moonshine still in one corner of the barn complete with jugs, empty fruit jars, and pipes everywhere.

The Brothers Four walked behind them with their guns raised expecting them to run away. Boss brother told Overalls Brother to put them in one of the stalls. He did and shut the door behind them. Boss Brother took off his hat and started beating Overalls Brother on the head. This wasn't the sharpest of the brothers, for sure.

"You didn't lock the door to that stall and didn't even tie them up. What were you thinking?" asked his disbelieving brother. "Get back in there and tie them up, Goofy."

"Yes Sir, you, overbearing, bossy, mean, stingy, hateful, brother," that's when the fun began. Boss brother picked up a shovel and knocked his brother over head with it while laughing when his brother fell like a two-year-old baby in the scattered hay on the floor of the barn.

The other two brothers must have felt left out, because they started fighting each other with fists and anything else they could find to hit each other with. It was a free-for-all in the old town tonight. The men in the stall couldn't believe what they were seeing, but it was fun to watch as long as they didn't come in their stall.

Fun was beginning to be stopped by a woman, who must be their mama, with an ugly looking expression and a large club in her hands. When the grown brothers saw their mama, they immediately stopped what they were doing.

"You idiots, I told you to get someone to help us build our shed, not kidnap a bunch of men. What is wrong with you? Every one of you are just like your poor ole dear departed sorry excuse of a dad. Now, come on in and get ready for bed," said the meanest mama in the universe.

"You boys in the stall, get a bunch of sleep, because you will need all the energy you can get to build our shed. I'll bring you something to eat shortly," said mommy dearest.

CHAPTER THIRTY-NINE

Sam awoke with a ghastly headache and confusion as to where he could be. After looking around, he couldn't figure it out. He saw multiple boxes stacked in one corner with shelves of what seemed to be linens and toilet paper. It had to be some kind of storage unit, but where. All places had storage units, so he could be anywhere. He hoped he was, at least, still in Texas, because he still wanted to find his wife.

He remembers being with Chad and Roy, but he can't remember anything after that. He reached up and rubbed his head that was still feeling atrocious and noticed he had a huge bump on the back of his head. After trying to stand up, he became extremely dizzy, so he sat back down on the hard floor before he fell on the concrete and did more damage to himself. He decided to sit and think about this strange situation.

He had a right to try to find his wife, didn't he? Why were Chad and Roy making it harder than it had to be? He knew they had searched for Charmaine, and he did also, but why can't anyone find her. She is big as a barrel and would be easy to notice. He still had hope he would get her back while he was here, if he ever got out of this weird room.

After looking around some more, he noticed a small table and a chair in the middle of the room. What he noticed the most was the food and bottles of water on the table. He was sure Chad and Roy had done that, as well as putting him here. He didn't know why they cared so much what happens with Charmaine. I'm just doing what I observed his dad doing to his mama.

He was more than angry. He wished Chad and Roy would come

here now. He would show them what they had done to him was wrong. When I get out of here, they are getting a dose of what I give Charmaine. I may have to kill them and throw them in here. That's when he fell back to sleep.

After a short nap, which helped his headache tremendously, he began thinking about what Chad and Roy have been trying to push in his clueless brain. Maybe they are right. Charmaine has never been anything, but nice to him. She may be late sometimes getting his supper on the table, but, at least, she always has supper for him every night. Now that he thinks more about the whole thing, she has only done nice things. This wasn't making him feel any better about beating her. He was thinking he could ask his cousins if they would help him know how to control his temper. Maybe my dad was wrong to beat my mama. It always made him mad at his dad when he hurt his mom, and here I am doing the same thing to my wife. He can't really blame Charmaine for running away from him.

CHAPTER FORTY

The crestfallen cousins trudged back to the dining area to search for the Dudes. They thought for sure they would be eating breakfast. They noticed they liked to eat a lot when they had eaten with them before. Maybe they aren't as hungry today, but they doubted that. At least, the rain had stopped during the night and the day was looking clear and sunny. They could hear a few voices, but most of the guests were, most likely, at one of the activities of the day.

The ladies hadn't had as much time as they wanted to think of what to do next. After Chad told them not to call the police, it seemed to be more of a dilemma to think of the right plan. One thing they knew they were going to do was search for the Dudes. They might need their help, and they were eager to help find Kiki and Charmaine.

Instead of the Dudes, they came upon Chad and Roy who didn't look too well this morning. They thought they might have had a wild night and just needed some rest. Maybe they came to find them so they could help. They could use all the help they could get with this situation.

"I'm going to tell you ladies something, but you can't tell anyone, okay?" explained a tire-eyed Chad, who began rubbing his head and eyes. His bad night was because he couldn't sleep because of worry about what they did to Sam. He was, after all, his and Roy's cousin, and he always believed that family should stick together.

"Your secret's safe with us. Go for it," said a happy Queenie. She felt they needed a secret to get them out of their doldrums. All the ladies were worried about the missing girls, but they would get it together in a bit and they would be ready to go again in their hunt for family. Actually, Kiki was the only family member, but they had sort of adopted Charmaine in their family too.

No one said anything for a moment, "Well, are you going to spell your secret or not?" asked Gigi whose curiosity was getting the better of her. They all were sitting on pins and needles waiting for Chad and Roy's secret. They all did love a good secret.

"Last night Sam had a little accident, and he is now locked in the basement of the registration building," said Roy with a weird expression on his tired face. Roy didn't know how the ladies were going to react about the awful thing they had done to Sam.

"I don't think you are telling us everything. We won't tell anyone. Go ahead and tell us," Bambi was getting irritated with their explanation. She thought they were leaving out some things, and they were.

"Last night we were having sort of an argument with Sam. Roy got aggravated and hit him over the head and knocked him out bad. We didn't know anything else to do but lock him in the basement. It seemed like a good plan at the time," said Chad while trying not to laugh at what they had done to poor ole Sam. As long as he wasn't dead, Chad was okay with what they did to Sam. Locking him in the basement was for the health of Chad and Roy. Sam was street-fighter tough and country strong.

"I think it was a noble gesture on you part. He deserves that and more for what he has done to his sweet wife," said an angry Jade. She didn't put up with mean people and thought what Chad and Roy did to Sam wasn't enough. There's no excuse to beat up your wife, especially if she's pregnant.

"I agree with you completely, but that wouldn't work," said Roy who would love to do to him what he did to Charmaine.

"Do the women of the world a favor and leave him there. I don't guess you would let us go in the basement room and persuade him to stop being abusive. We promise not to hurt him too bad," said Bambi with a mammoth smile. All the gentile ladies had huge smiles on their faces when Bambi came up with her idea, who thought that was a wonderful thing to think of.

"Maybe it will all work out. Sam told Roy and me he was thinking about giving her a divorce and find him a tougher wife," related Chad while shaking his head like he couldn't believe what Sam had told him and his brother.

Olivia gazed at the others and said, "I'm not very fond of divorce, but in this case, it might be the best outcome, or we could get Tinker and her ball bat ahold of him. Olivia was smiling extra huge now just thinking about Tinker being in a room with her ball bat and Charmaine's husband. The cousins were not horrible people, but they thought Sam needed to be punished.

"Let's go, girls. We need to find the Dudes," said Queenie, who was anxious to get the day started.

"I can help you ladies with that. I saw them after breakfast this morning heading toward where the activities were going on," said Roy.

"Thanks, Roy. Y'all take care," smiled Gigi.

CHAPTER FORTY-ONE

C had had to return to work, so he wouldn't lose his job. Although, if his boss found out he had put a man in the basement with the supplies, his job may not last very long at all. They would have to let Sam out eventually but needed to wait until the time was right. He thought maybe one day he and Roy could go down there and try to talk some sense in him. There was a fifty/fifty chance it would work, but they had to try. His mom always said that boy would wind up being good for nothing. She knew what he does to Charmaine, and thought it was the most horrible thing she had ever heard. Sam's dad had done that to her, but her secret was that she kept her iron skillet in a place she could get to easily, and every time he beat on her, she gave back as more than she got.

"Ladies, I have to return to work, but you can have Roy. He's a good tracker and can protect you," smiled Chad hoping they would find Charmaine before she decided to have that baby.

"Bye, Chad. We need to get started with our mission. We'll break up and find our helpers. The more we can get, the better. Tinker should be the easiest one to find. We now know where her cabin is located. Angel and Olivia, why don't you go to Tinker's cabin and bring her back with you," said Queenie with a smile that could light up the world.

"Oh no, no, no," hollered Angel. They all thought her adventure with Tinker's pigs and chickens had her spooked a bit. They would tease her later about baby pigs and foot high chickens chasing her around Tinker's cabin.

Queenie glance at Olivia, "What about you, girl? Your cow

incident wasn't too bad, was it? You got to see the loft in Tinker's barn and a nice bale of sticky hay to sit on and rest.

Olivia responded with a smile, "Maybe you can give us a different job."

"Okay, Jade and Bambi can go get Tinker. If we had her cell phone number, it would be easier, but I'm not sure she has a cell phone. Take Roy with you for protection from the pigs, chickens, the cow, and maybe that big mongrel named Susie," Queenie smiled and thought she had a good idea this time.

Trixie looked at the bossy Queenie and asked, "What do you want Gigi and I to do. We want to help."

"Your job is to see if you can find the Dudes. Chad said he saw them go toward the activities, so that shouldn't be too hard to do. Let's gather back here at the dining area," said bossy butt Queenie. Trixie and Gigi laughed all the way to the activities.

"The rest of us will stay here and think of a plan," Olivia was happy she wasn't going to have to go to Tinker's cabin. She would rather be here thinking than being chased by a large animal in the rustic barn of Tinker's. She wasn't too fond of that monster dog of hers either. He looked like he ate small children for supper. Maybe that's why she hasn't seen a small child since they arrived here at the Dude Ranch.

Trixie and Gigi headed toward where the activities of the day were. There were all kinds of fun stuff to do, but they finally found the Dudes at the roping class. They didn't seem to be doing too well. Every time Little Dude threw the rope, he hit another person who was the closest to him. The rope didn't go around that person but would often hit them in the face or other parts of their body. B Dude wasn't much better. He was aiming at a horse, but the rope knocked one of the ranch hands off his wagon. Trixie and Gigi were having a grand ole time watching the Dudes try their hand at roping. They should keep their day jobs whatever that was.

"Let's go get them before they kill somebody with the rope. Anybody could beat them at roping, even my ninety-year-old great grandmother," smiled Trixie as she noticed Gigi laughing at the uncoordinated men. They thought they did much better at roping than the Dudes were doing. They had no coordination at all.

"What do you girls think about our roping skills?" asked B Dude as he smiled at Gigi, who was afraid they might ask that question. She had to think of something quick.

"Wow, boys. I don't have enough words to explain how well you did," lied a giggling Gigi. She didn't want to hurt their feelings, but they had to know they wouldn't win a rodeo contest. You don't knock a ranch hand off his wagon in a rodeo contest.

Trixie smiled big at the Dudes and Gigi, "Let's go do what we came here to do. Follow us Dudes. We have work to do. Roping is over for the day. Maybe you will be able to do it another day, not that you need the practice. You don't, but you never know how much better a man could get if he roped often."

"You are so right," said Little Dude. "We will take that under consideration." The Dudes were happy the nice ladies talked to them and wanted their help. They would do anything for them.

CHAPTER FORTY-TWO

The unhappy ranch hand began waking his prisoners with an aggressive shake to the shoulder. Kiki awoke immediately, but it took Charmaine longer. The baby was probably making her more tired than Kiki. Charmaine squinted at the sun beams in the opening of their jail. The girls were confused and wondered if he was going to let them go, since he wanted them to wake up so quickly. Kiki didn't think that was the plan, but it didn't hurt to have good expectations rather than bad ones. With this man, it couldn't be anything but bad, because he had told her the story about his parents killing his sister. Kiki didn't know if that story was true or not, but something made him mad as a hatter at the world, so it could be true.

"Where are you taking us?" asked Kiki who was filled with curiosity. "You know that we need to go slow wherever it is you are taking us, because Charmaine is a little slower these days with the baby weighing her down. Jesus would want you to be considerate of a pregnant woman and be nice to everyone. Killing people is wrong, wrong, wrong. Jesus loves everybody and that includes you. You should be better to people. It's not too late for you to stop this awful thing you are doing and live a better life. You seem to like your job, so why not be happy. Find you a good woman and have a good life instead of sitting in a prison for the rest of your life."

"Did anybody ever tell you that you talk too much? Do you ever shut up?" asked the agitated ranch hand while rubbing his head in frustration.

He pushes the ladies out the door of the dark cave. They couldn't see at first because the bright sunshine was hurting their eyes. He waited patiently while the girls got themselves together. After the ranch hand thought they had enough time to get used to the sun shining down on them, he pushed them again in the direction he wanted them to go. The entire time they walked, he kept his gun raised at their backs. Kiki walked right behind Charmaine, so if the disturbed man was going to shoot someone, she didn't want it to be the young expectant mother.

Kiki suddenly notice the cabin where her cousins and her went to and found the weird little door underneath the cabin. Her mind was thinking overtime, and that's when it hit her. The noise through the little door could have been a woman someone had put there, and that was her way of letting them know she was there and could they help her. Instead, the cousins were a little frightened, so they ran away instead of checking further. That thought made Kiki feel bad. Maybe they could have saved the woman. The scream they heard was certainly someone who was hurting. This wasn't going to turn out well.

The ranch hand pushed them again to get them to go up the steps to the door of the cabin. The girls walked slowly giving themselves more time before he did whatever he was going to do to the ladies. Kiki wasn't too sure Charmaine could handle the steps down underground. There were steps missing and she sure didn't need to fall down them. She was weak from not enough food and was a little top-heavy.

"Can we sit down in these two chairs here in the living room and rest. We walked a long way and need to relax a moment. You can, at least, give us a few minutes," said Kiki who was getting aggravated herself. She knew whatever he was going to do was not going to turn out good for them. She started exaggerating her breathing so he might let them sit before taking them farther.

"Okay, but don't expect me to make you a four-course meal. Just sit there and think about food," he seemed to be getting to the point of anger again, but he was a man who was angry at the world.

"Charmaine is eating for two. At least, give her some food, even if it's only a cracker," pleaded a concerned Kiki. "Why couldn't you have brought us here last night, so we could have had better shelter?"

"Yep, you talk too much," he said this as he slapped Kiki across the mouth making her mouth bleed.

Charmaine was crying when she saw the blood on Kiki's mouth. Kiki didn't want to upset Charmaine, so she smiled when she noticed Charmaine looking at the blood. Of course, her teeth were red, but at least, Kiki smiled at her and said, "I'm okay. It's hard to get a good woman down. Don't spend your time worrying about me." Kiki was trying to think of something to do that might help them survive. She didn't know what they could be, but it wouldn't stop her from trying.

Charmaine whispered to Kiki, "Maybe you shouldn't make him mad by talking too much." This made Kiki smile for Charmaine to be concerned about her.

"I'm trying to buy us some time, so my cousins will be able to find us. They know this cabin. We were here before, and they are smart enough to figure out where we are," smiled Kiki still with bright red teeth.

"I have some questions for you. Are you crazy? What do you intend to do with us? Did you kill the woman propped against the tree? If you did kill her, why did you do it?" Kiki knew she was trying his patience, but she wanted to kill some more time. "Let's bow our heads. Dear Heavenly Father, we thank you for all our blessings and praise your Holy name. We pray, Lord, you will forgive this man for what he had done and what's he's about to do. I pray he can change his life of crime and be a happy man. Lord, give Charmaine and me the strength to get through this awful situation. It wouldn't hurt our feelings if a snake bit this horrible man. We ask these things in your precious name. Amen."

The disgruntled ranch hand put his hands over his ears. She went too far this time. She is the crazy one, "Shut up, woman. Yes, I killed her. She deserved it. She looked kind of like my mom."

"That's not a good reason to kill another human being. Maybe you are a crazy man!" said a cautious Kiki who knew he wouldn't like what she said, and he possibly would take his anger out on her again. Kiki didn't mind just so he wasn't doing it to Charmaine.

Kiki was right. He didn't like what she had to say one little bit. As he was talking, he pushed her chair over backwards making her bang her head on the way down. That's when he put his foot on her neck and told her to never call him crazy again, or he would kill her after he tortured her first. He knew several good tortures because of his dearly departed parents.

That's when Kiki smiled again at Charmaine to let her know she was alright. Kiki smiled at the young mother-to-be and whispered, "Don't you say anything to this loony man."

Charmaine knew what Kiki meant, so she decided to do as Kiki said to protect her baby from harm. Protecting her baby was Charmaine's main goal right now.

What the captive ladies didn't know was that the ranch hand was having second thoughts about what he was about to do. Being happy all the time would be great. He could be a good man if he wanted to. His parents never took them to church, but he had heard others talk about Jesus before, and that He was good and just. He would have to think some more about this or maybe talk to the mouthy one who couldn't seem to keep quiet. Maybe I could start out by not killing the ladies, but just torture them. He thought that was a good plan.

CHAPTER FORTY-THREE

The shed-building boys in the barn didn't sleep too well wondering how they got in this insane situation. It wasn't quite as bad as being a cattle rustler, but it wasn't pleasant all the same. There wasn't much room in the stall they put the boys in, because it wasn't too big, and they were big strapping men. At least, it had lots of hay to lay on, which was not made for a good night's sleep.

"I'm itching all over and sneezing like crazy," said an unhappy Forrest as he glanced at the others to see if they were scratching. If he got out of here, he vowed to never sleep on hay again in his lifetime.

The unlucky men were trying to think of how they could get out of this old dingy barn. The fumes from the moonshine still was almost enough to make a man have a small buzz. Before they could think too much, they heard the double barn doors slowly open with an old woman in a ragged dress, and her gray hair up in a bun on top of her head. The only good thing about her was the basket of biscuits she was carrying on her left arm.

"Alright, you lazy boys are probably hungry as a pig. I am giving you some biscuits so you will have some energy to build our shed. We are calling it our moonshine shed, because we have got to get this still out of the barn. It makes the cows woozy to smell our brew, plus we wouldn't want the barn to burn while we were brewing our shine. Then we would be up a creek without a paddle. We depend on this money to live a good life. My boys haven't had a dad around to teach them to do stuff, so we have to get outside help, and you're it," explained the boss of this outfit.

"No, I guess that would be bad for your barn to burn, but why can't your hire someone from town to build your shed?" asked a curious Stonewall.

"My boys are tender and extremely tender-hearted. I wouldn't want them to get hurt trying to build the shed. You men seem to be sturdy enough. My boys are just so precious, so I won't let them do too much around here," explained the insane women with the biscuits. They didn't want to make her mad.

Stone didn't say anything to that asinine statement the old woman just made, because if she didn't like what he said, she wouldn't leave that basket of biscuits and they were hungry, "Don't you think it's wrong to make moonshine, Ma'am?"

"No, no," stated old lady. "I'm from Georgia and my granddaddy made moonshine out in the woods, so I taught my boys how to make it, so they would have a good job opportunity and get money for themselves. I'm not going to be around forever, and they need to learn a trade."

The precious boys walked into the barn while their mom was explaining about her granddaddy and moonshine, "Our mama taught us right, and we came out okay," explained the oldest one who did all the talking.

"Yes, Sir, you did okay for yourselves. Actually, I'm from Georgia, and my granddaddy made moonshine with a friend of his before I was born. It wasn't right for him to make the shine either, but he finally saw the error of his ways. He had to stop when my cousin threw rocks at his fruit jars and broke them all. We didn't think she had it in her to hit the jars, but she proved us wrong, true story," explained Stone. He thought if they knew his granddaddy made shine, then they would let them go away from here and not have to build their shed for them.

Beau whispered in Stone's ear, "About her boys coming out okay is debatable. I don't think they have but one good brain between all four of them."

Stone began to chuckle lightly so as not to be heard before saying, "Shh. Let's don't make them mad. We might not get our hard biscuit in the morning. Wasn't that the hardest biscuit you have ever had? You're right about the brain, but at least they are learning a trade, since they are so precious," laughed Stone.

"You forget, Beau, when our little sister made her first batch of biscuits. You could have knocked a bobcat out of a tree with it and kill that bobcat stone dead," Stone thought it was funny, but little sister didn't think it was so funny at the time, but you can bet they never let her live it down.

The men told them to stop talking as they opened the stall door where they had almost got a few minutes sleep the night before. When they got outside, they noticed the old hound dog sleeping on the hard ground. Old Turd sure was a good guard dog. Mama's precious boys walked the working men behind a huge rock where the shed would be built. The brother without front teeth had to pick up old Turd to take him with them, because the dog never woke up at all, even when he was being carried.

Mama walked out to where the shed was to be built, so she could make sure they got started. She frowned at the working men and said, "If you try to run away, Turd will find you and it won't be pretty what he does to you yahoos," As the men watched mama walk away, they looked down at old Turd, who seemed to still be in dreamland. They weren't too worried about their guard dog.

CHAPTER FORTY-FOUR

Jade, Bambi, and Roy ambled on toward Tinker Bell's cabin through brush and brambles until they saw the cabin that surprised them that it was still standing. It hadn't changed much since they had breakfast there. At least, they didn't see that mammoth dog that washed the dishes. He was scary, and they weren't sure that he didn't eat people on occasion. Most of them had never seen a dog that huge in person before, and they didn't care if they saw one again.

The closer they got to the cabin they could see that everything was quiet with no animals running around the yard. Maybe this was going to be a happy visit. Jade couldn't understand why the girls ran from chickens and pigs earlier. They were little pigs, and Angel was much taller than they were. She can understand Olivia and the cow. The cow was much bigger than she was. Looks like they won't have that problem this time. All was good.

Suddenly out came the chickens, cow, and pigs making noises as if they were saying, "Oh boy, the crazy humans are back. Let's chase them around the house so we can get a good laugh."

They heard a squeak and turned toward the barn where the barn's double doors were slowly opening to let the cow out in the yard. Jade walked to the cow, patted her on the back and went back to Bambi who was staying her distance from all the animals. The cow turned around and went back in the barn. Maybe that's all the cow wanted was to have some attention. The cow must be deprived of human love. They would have to tell Olivia about their experience with the cow at Tinker Bell's.

While they were watching the huge cow, Roy was being chased

around the house by the chickens and pigs. Roy was doing ok until he tripped over a chicken and fell on the hard ground and broke his arm.

While holding his arm, Roy said, "Those are demon pigs and chickens. They are rough on a good man." Jade and Bambi didn't want to laugh just in case his arm was really broken, but it was hard to refrain.

Tinker was watching all the commotion outside in her yard hardly able to control her laughter. She loved it when her chickens and pigs chase people around the house. She had to get her jollies somewhere and this was great. Tinker loved it when company came. It was a good security system when the pigs squealed, the chickens clucked, and the cow bellowed, and she knew when someone was outside her house

Tinker Bell finally made it outside with her ball bat and the male dog named Susie. The ball bat was okay with the others, but the dog, not so much. Tinker knew why they were here, so she could help them find the two that were missing. She wanted to help all she could. It wouldn't be right for her not to help. She didn't like at all what they said that Charmaine's husband did to her. If someone took them, Lord, be with the one who gets on the top end of Tinker's ball bat. No telling what that monster dog would do to them. Then she took out some material to make Roy a sling for his arm from his chicken and pig fiasco.

CHAPTER FORTY-FIVE

The hateful ranch hand goes to see what's in the other room. He wasn't worried about the ladies trying to escape. They had to be tired after all that walking to get here to the cabin. There is the fact that the pregnant one probably can't run too fast anyway. He was looking at everything in every room to see if there was anything he could use. The cabin was mostly bare in the rooms except for small stuff. He would have to make do with what he already had down under the cabin.

He was way off track if he thought the ladies wouldn't try to run away. Kiki whispered quietly to Charmaine, "Walk quietly toward the door. After we slowly get off the porch, let's run as fast as possible. Don't worry. I'll help you if you need me to."

"Okay, I'll do it. Running is better than what he has in mind for us. I used to run track in high school. I'm a little weighted down right now, but I'll give it all I can," smiled a very pregnant Charmaine.

"Good girl," said Kiki as they slowly made their way to the door and down the steps of the front porch. Kiki said a little prayer as they began to run.

Kiki began talking to her running mate while they were hightailing it down a small hill, "Let's run back to the cave to rest a bit. It's close to the ranch. We get there, pray first, and then we run like the dickens toward the ranch and find help."

"Good idea, Kiki. I don't know what I would do without your help. Thank you so much," said Charmaine with a rapid heartbeat. "I may have to name my baby after you."

"Don't you think a baby boy named Kiki would be a little weird?" laughed Kiki who was glad she was here to help her all she could.

Charmaine laughed along with Kiki, "I guess I would have to re-think names if it was a boy."

"There's the cave. Go inside quickly. I have been afraid to look back to see if he was following us, but now that I can look, I don't see him," Kiki was breathing hard and needed a minute to get her heart rate down before even trying to run to the ranch, but she didn't want to wait very long. They didn't have much time to waste.

CHAPTER FORTY-SIX

The tired ranch hand finished his survey of the rest of the cabin and came up with nothing that could help him. He went back to the living room to find the crazy ladies gone. He really didn't think they had it in them, but he figured if they were scared enough, they would do anything to get away. He wondered how the pregnant woman made it. She probably had to stop and rest a lot, so that would give him an advantage. It wasn't good for them to make him angry.

He knew he had to think about where they would go to get away from him. The ranch would be the most logical place, but then again, he thinks they would go to the cave because they would need a rest. He will try the cave first. He would bring them back to the cabin even if he had to drag them by the hair.

He walks out of the rustic cabin and down the front porch steps. He can't see any footprints except the ones they made coming to the cabin. He had to give them credit. They were good, but they weren't as smart as him, so he didn't worry too much. He didn't want to get caught. He wanted to keep his job at the ranch and maybe give up the killing thing. Maybe Kiki made somewhat of an impression on him. She seemed to believe in him and that he could be better.

He really didn't know why he was still doing this to women. He had done more than enough to have revenge on his parents that he killed, because they killed his twin sister. He always took care of her, because she was so frail and was not as strong as he was. It broke his heart when he saw them kill her, but mostly the anger in him wouldn't seem to go away. Maybe he should stop, and now would be a good time to stop right after he killed these two who could identify him. Then he would stop and have somewhat of a normal life.

He keeps thinking about the lady who was pregnant and how happy she must be to be having a baby. He was sort of taking her joy right now, and that didn't make him feel good, although, she can identify him as well as the other one can. Yep, he must get these women back before he stops doing this awful thing.

First, I need to find them. I'll go to the cave first.

CHAPTER FORTY-SEVEN

After gathering the cousins, Roy, the Dude brothers, and Tinker Bell, they began to think of what to do next. They sat quietly at the table while finishing their BBQ lunch. The tired girls thought about Charmaine and Kiki and if they had any food. Charmaine needed food since she was eating for two now. Even if they had food, they knew Kiki would give hers to Charmaine because that was the kind of person she was.

"We need to think first of scenarios of what could have happened to them," said Roy after being looked at by the ranch doctor who said it was only a sprain was still worried about Charmaine. He didn't like the way his cousin, Sam, treated her and felt sorry for her. Roy's mom and dad thought it was horrible what Sam did to Charmaine, but they didn't think they could do anything. Praying was all they could do.

"Do you think that Charmaine may have gotten lost, and Kiki decided to go by herself to find her?" asked Angel who was worried for about both women.

Olivia spoke, "I don't think Kiki would go off by herself, especially with her hurt ankle. She knows it's best to wait to walk on it until there isn't much soreness. If she didn't wait, I'll get her good when I see her." They knew Olivia wouldn't do anything bad to anyone, so they weren't worried.

"That leaves the fact that someone must have taken them," Jade's idea was met with more worried glances, because it could be true. "He could have taken Charmaine first and later saw Kiki and took her too." Jade was hoping that wasn't the case, but it was certainly a possibility.

Jade's idea made them all think this could have easily been what happened. Someone had to have taken that poor woman they found dead propped against a tree. That didn't make the motley group feel much better, but she was right. It is possible that is what happened.

"Okay, let's say this is what went down. Where do you think they would take them?" asked Queenie in a curious manner.

"My first guess would be the old cabin we went in. Remember the underground door and the sound we heard? That could have been the woman that was found dead by the tree," Gigi was making sense. She wished she wasn't right, but it was looking more like that was what had happened.

"I say we go to the cabin. I've got my ball bat ready, and Susie will do what I tell him to do," said Tinker who appeared not to be able to wait for some action. The others knew that Tinker was going to come in handy, and she was one who would do stuff they wouldn't even think of. Tinker was sitting on ready.

"I think we are all ready to search that old cabin. Let's hit it," hollered Gigi with more excitement they had ever seen in her. She was ready to get the ladies back.

While traveling to the rustic cabin, they met one of the ranch hands coming from where the cabin was located. Of course, he had a right to be there since he was an employee of the ranch. They couldn't accuse him of anything, because they didn't know anything for sure.

He glanced at the big group, "Hi, you out getting some exercise?" said the ranch hand. The others wondered why he would be out there when he had a job to do at the ranch.

Queenie quickly spoke up first, "Yes, we are. It's such a pretty day, don't you think?" The ranch hand smiled at the ladies and walked on toward the main part of the ranch.

"Sure is. Be careful. There could be snakes or bobcats," replied the man who was wondering why that many people were getting their exercise together. It made him think about what they were really out here for. He began to become a touch worried. He knew the last one he took today was with the ladies of that group. He couldn't worry about that now. He had to find out where his captives were.

Angel ran up to Gigi and stood close. She wasn't really a snake person, but then again, who was? Gigi knew why she was beside her. They all knew Angel had a huge fear of snakes. Let's face it. No one likes snakes, but Angel's fear was astronomical.

Gigi looked at Angel, "You know he was teasing us, and it makes me wonder why. It was like he was trying to scare us into going back to the ranch.

The others had their doubts too, but they had to get their mind back on their mission. The group of hopeful people who wanted to find their friends walked to the cabin and went through the front door. After searching all the rooms, they knew they all couldn't fit in the small area down the ladder.

Queenie spoke in her bossy way, "Tinker, Roy, and the Dudes go down and look on the other side of the small door while Gigi and I will wait outside the door to help in case they need to take anything upstairs. The others stay alert and maybe search outside the cabin."

"Alright then, that's a good plan. Let's go, girls," said Trixie with eagerness in her voice while walking toward the cabin door with her trusty shovel in her hand.

CHAPTER FORTY-EIGHT

Kiki and Charmaine felt better after resting for a while. Charmaine smiled at Kiki and asked what they needed to do, because she thought this cave might be the first place the ranch hand may look. She was right, and she was ready to fight to save her baby.

Kiki agreed with her, and she had been thinking along the same lines as Charmaine. They needed, for sure, to find another hiding place. They decided to start walking and look for a place to hide along the way. There had to be more places to hide besides in this cave.

The run-a-way ladies walked for a while and finally found a place as they looked up in a tree with a deer stand. There was a ladder and Kiki worried if Charmaine could get up to the stand way up in the tree, even with a ladder. She was sure her large baby belly would get in her way.

Charmaine must have noticed the indecision on Kiki's sweet face, "Kiki, don't worry about me. I would go up a ladder higher than that one to save my baby. Let's give that ladder a try."

Kiki told Charmaine to go up first and she would be right behind her, so up they went to the top. When they finally made it up to the top, they found a camouflage tarp, that they were afraid a snake could be under it, to cover them. Things were looking up some for the escapees. It wasn't comfortable, but they couldn't think about that.

"Listen, I hear footsteps coming this way," said Kiki with her keen sense of hearing. She observed the area around them quickly and saw someone who had to be the one they were running away from walking slowly toward them. She didn't know if he had seen them yet. He may not look up while searching for them. Who would think a large pregnant woman would climb up in a treestand.

"Here, put this tarp over us. When we're under the tarp, stay completely still and no talking or even loud breathing." Kiki got them in a position to look like it was just a pile of camouflage tarp.

They could hear the footsteps coming closer, and for a few minutes, the steps stopped. Whoever it was turned slightly and walked away. The ladies stayed in their current position until they thought whoever it was had to be far enough away from them, but then they needed to do it slowly just in case.

The tired ladies felt it was, for sure, the ranch hand who had taken them that had been stopped by the tree stand. He must have thought a pregnant lady wouldn't have gone up a ladder that tall. What Charmaine said next to Kiki surprised her. Charmaine told her she was afraid of high places.

"Honey, you are a remarkable woman. Some women wouldn't climb up that high on that homemade ladder even if they weren't pregnant," They both started laughing at Kiki's words making them feel much better about this whole situation. A little laughter was what they needed to give them hope of not being taken again.

Eventually, the tree house ladies came out of their tree when they thought the coast was clear. After getting the kinks out of their legs from sitting still for so long, they began looking around for another place to hide.

"You know, I'm pretty sure the dining area of the ranch is over to our left. We could go there and search around for the girls. Wouldn't it be nice to meet up with them? They probably have the Dude brothers with them and they, most likely, are looking for us," explained Kiki who thought this was a great plan.

"What makes you think your cousins will be out looking for you?" asked a confused Charmaine. She couldn't imagine why they would be going to such trouble to find them.

"Sweety, trust me. They are out looking. Family takes care of each other, and my cousins I'm with here at the ranch are special and would scale up a tall building like Spiderman rather than not look for kin," explained Kiki to a smiling Charmaine who would love to have lots of cousins who help her. If she did, she would love to see what they would do to Sam. What Charmaine didn't know was that Sam's cousins were taking up for her, and they have Sam in a place right now where he can't hurt her.

"I trust you, girl. I can't think of anything different to do, except we need to stay in the shadows and a little prayer wouldn't hurt either. Our captor may be here looking around for us," stated Charmaine with a good point. Charmaine knew she was fortunate to have Kiki here to help her through this whole encounter.

"You're right. We need to be super careful. Getting caught is not a good option for us. I'll protect you as much as I can. You have become a good friend," said Kiki with a sweet smile.

CHAPTER FORTY-NINE

As he left the antiquated cabin, the ranch hand had thoughts of what he would do with the run-a-way girls. He didn't take them for being runners. The one with the big belly looking like she may drop a baby any minute surely didn't look like a runner. His grandmother used to tell him that looks can be deceiving. He was thinking she may have been right about that.

He often wished when he was a kid having to live with abusive parents, why his grandmother didn't come and take his sister and him home with her, but that's in the past. He knew he needed to stop living in the past. His sister wouldn't be happy with him if she was still alive to see what he has done. Maybe it was time to stop hurting women and be a decent man. He had a job he liked and might find him a wife and have a kid or two one day. He decided this would be the last time he would torture and kill women who didn't have a thing to do with his past. These two women he was searching for could identify him, and that was not good, he would catch them and finish his job.

His musings stopped as he noticed he was nearing the cave where he had first taken the ladies. He walked softly as he crept to the opening of the cave, so he wouldn't scare them into doing something he wouldn't like. They may have found a big stick just waiting for him to come in and hit him over the head. He didn't know about the pregnant one, but the other one was sassy. He wouldn't put it past her to hit him with a stick.

Going inside the cave made him relieved to see they were not there, and he wouldn't be hit over the head. He wondered where they went. If they went back to the cabin, he would have met them. Maybe they went to the ranch.

As he left the cave, he walked in the direction of the ranch. He met up with the ladies that the sassy one came with for the week. He didn't like this at all. He felt they may have been looking for the two he took. This can't be good. He didn't think about somebody hunting the ladies. He didn't understand why they were looking for them.

He trotted on toward the ranch. He needed to put in another appearance anyway, so he wouldn't lose his job. That's when he noticed a tree with a deer stand. All he could see was an old camouflage tarp. He didn't think the crazy women were up that high. Who ever heard of a pregnant woman climbing a tree? Most women who were not pregnant would climb that high. He stopped and listened and observed. After not hearing or seeing anything, he thought they were heading toward the ranch, and that's exactly what he would do.

CHAPTER FIFTY

Trixie shooed the rest of the women out the door of the old cabin. She was so excited, she jumped off the tall porch while the ones on the porch stood with mouths hanging open right before they broke into bouts of laughter. They hesitated about laughing to make sure Trixie wasn't hurt. She was okay, so they could laugh about it. Trixie was ready to get started with her mission of checking the outside of the cabin, "Jump on down here. It's a hoot." That's when Trixie began singing and dancing, while the others looked on in amazement. They thought 'why not' and that's when they all jumped on the hard ground and started dancing with Trixie.

"Come on, lovely ladies. Let's go around to the back yard first," said Trixie as she led them to the back. They wondered what had gotten into their cousin. Maybe it's from the fear of their cousin being taken to who knows where, or it could be the two pieces of cake she had earlier. Trixie always had a tendency to be somewhat hyper when eating sugar. It didn't keep her from singing and dancing all the way to the back yard. The other cousins followed right behind dancing all the way.

They searched for something out of the ordinary in the back yard, but they came up with nothing unusual. The only thing they saw was empty coke cans and Honey Bun wrappers.

"That is not really suspicious. Could have been kids hanging around. They would come more throwing their trash down on the ground instead of putting it in a trash can," said Angel with a smile at her cousins. "We need to go check out the front yard. We didn't see anything unusual, but you never know what we may find if we look closely."

"You're right, Angel. I'm ready. I wonder how the others are doing under the cabin. We haven't heard any screaming, so I guess they're alright," Olivia made good sense, but she was a little concerned about why they haven't come out yet.

Bambi looked at the other and said, "What do we do if we hear screaming from down there?" Bambi saw a big stick and picked it up, because she wanted to be prepared if they hear screaming. So far, so good. Maybe they were okay.

"I guess we find us a stick too and go look if that happens," said Jade who probably didn't need a stick. She's handy in a crisis.

"Shh. Listen. Do you hear that?" asked Jade who had an unusual expression on her face. The others couldn't make out what her look could mean.

Jade walked closer to the front porch and squatted down to look under the high porch. The other cousins had various looks of confusion all over their faces. They knew Jade liked to tease them sometimes, so they weren't too worried. They thought Jade must be deranged and watched as she slowly stood straight up.

"What did you see under there, girl? Spit it out," said a laughing Bambi. That's when they heard a growl. "It might be time to go back in the cabin."

Jade looked at the curious women and said, "All I saw was eyeballs. It's too dark to see what kind of animal it is, but apparently, we all have a big stick. If it's an animal, it's only one, because I didn't see but one set of eyes."

"Don't leave me," said whatever was under the porch. They thought that knocked the animal theory out of the water.

"Help me get whoever it is out from under there," said Jade as she squatted again.

They all squatted and watched as the pair of eyes came closer to the edge of the porch. What came out was a girl, who may have been around thirteen years old. They helped her stand up and noticed her clothes were extremely dirty along with her long brown hair which was matted horribly. They didn't know if it would be able to be brushed out or not. It was pretty bad.

Bambi told the others they were going to need to help her up. She was sort of stuck in the squatting position. Jade went over and pulled her up. But Bambi wasn't the only one who couldn't get up. Angel was asking for help also, so Jade went to help her get up. Jade looked at the others to see if they had gotten up, and all was well.

"Sweetheart, what's your name?" asked Trixie with her big smile. They were all confused and wanted to know what her story was.

"My name is Jennifer Cheyenne, ma'am, but you can just call me Cheyenne. The girl gave a small smile to the nice women. She felt she could trust them. "I don't live at home anymore."

Trixie was still wanting to know more, "Why were you under the porch, Honey?"

Cheyenne hung her head in embarrassment, "I live under there ma'am." That brought tears to Trixie's eyes. They really needed to find her another place to live. Surely someone around here would take her in. She would talk to the others about all this later after they found Charmaine and Kiki.

"Would you tell us how you came to live here?" Jade couldn't believe what she had found. She sure didn't start out this morning thinking that she would find a young girl living under the porch of a cabin.

"About a year ago, my mama told my daddy he had to leave and not come back. She said he had syphilis. I didn't know what that meant, but I have an Aunt Phillis. I figured he must have had an affair with her. You know, the names sounding alike and all. I loved my daddy something fierce, and I hated to see him go, but he told me he would write me a letter and tell him where he was. That was somewhat confusing to me because my daddy couldn't write a lick."

"Anyway, he's gone, and mama made it clear she didn't want to see him ever again in this dang old house. When Aunt Phillis heard what mama had done to daddy, she came over with Ethel."

"Who is Ethel?" asked Bambi who was listening intently. She thought this was better than going to a movie and immensely entertaining.

"Ethel is Aunt Phillis's old shotgun she inherited from her dear departed Grandpa," said Cheyenne. That statement made several pairs of eyes go wide and small giggles pursued.

"Aunt Phillis aimed Ethel at my mama and started shooting at her, because she wanted to shoot mama deader than Uncle Henry. Thank goodness, Aunt Phillis was cross-eyed and was a lousy shot."

"Mama ran behind the barn, slipped, and fell face first in the pig poop. She's never was the same again. Every day she just sits in her old rocker on the front porch and sings, *"Here Piggy, Piggy, Here Piggy, Piggy.* It was so sad, I left home. I don't live at home anymore."

"How about we find you a nice home?" asked Trixie wiping her tearful eyes from the laughter. They all had giggled or laughed a little, but they didn't let it show to Cheyenne, but it was such a wild story. They didn't want to hurt her feelings, but then Cheyenne started laughing right along with them. She like happy people who liked to laugh.

CHAPTER FIFTY-ONE

Queenie and Gigi waited patiently for Roy, the Dude brothers, and Tinker to finish with their search. They couldn't understand what was taking them so long. The ladies were wondering what they might have found behind the small mysterious door. They hoped they had enough light, so they could see what was really going on in that dark place. They didn't think they had found Kiki or Charmaine, or they would be out here by now.

The small door opened with solemn people slowly walking out of the room. Even Susie was hanging his head. This couldn't be anything but bad.

"You won't believe what we found, and it wasn't good," said Roy while shaking his head with a look of disbelief written all over his face. He seemed to about to cry.

Queenie and Gigi didn't really want to know what they found, but they were curious enough to let them go ahead and tell them.

"Tinker tell us what you found," stated Queenie, who could tell by their faces, they only found the bad stuff.

"Okay, we found what appeared to be a torture chamber," when Tinker said that, Queenie and Gigi's faces turned snow white.

Tinker saw their faces, "We didn't see any evidence that Charmaine or Kiki has been here." The girls believed her, because if they had been there, they knew Kiki would have found a way to leave some sort of clue. She was intelligent and would have done something. Kiki knew they would be searching for her without a doubt.

"There's more. There were heavy chains with metal bands that would fit over wrists and ankles. There was also cigarette butts and empty shell casings from a gun on the floor, and we saw blood on the floor and on the chains." Tinker didn't like having to upset her new friends, but she thought these two women were strong and could handle it.

They all walked outside to see the others who were waiting to hear what they found. The ones who were already outside noticed Charmaine or Kiki weren't with them. Tinker told them exactly what she had told Queenie and Gigi.

Tinker noticed the new addition to the group, "Cheyenne?"

Jennifer Cheyenne ran to Tinker and gave her a big Texas hug. The rest of the group was surprised at this change of events.

"What are you doing here, girl?" asked a curious Tinker.

"I sort of live under the porch." Cheyenne told Tinker the same story she told the others. Tinker was taking this all in with a frown on her face.

"Your Aunt Phillis never was a good shot. She really needs to look into getting those eyes fixed," said Tinker who was looking Jennifer Cheyenne up and down before saying, "You are not going back under that porch. You will come live with me as long as you want. I haven't seen you in a coon's age, girl."

"Thanks, Tinker," said Cheyenne as she started jumping up and down. The others were laughing right along with her.

"Hey, y'all. Tinker has always been one of my favorite people, and I'm going to get to live with her," The group in the yard of the cabin were smiling and laughing at Cheyenne's exuberant attitude. They were glad she wouldn't have to live under the porch anymore.

CHAPTER FIFTY-TWO

K iki and Charmaine carefully went down the ladder to the ground below. It was high, but doable. Kiki went down first, so she could catch Charmaine in case she fell. It had to be better to fall on a person than the hard ground. They knew the next thing they did was critical. Since the ranch hand went to the ranch, they would have to be on the lookout continually when walking around. Getting caught by him wasn't exactly what they wanted to happen. They made it down with no accidents and headed in the direction of the ranch.

Kiki was right about the direction to the barn. They found a tree to hid behind until they could find a good place to hide. Going from tree to tree seemed to last forever. It seemed no time at all, they were beside the big barn where they noticed a small shed where they may keep supplies. It was a better place to hide than the barn. After going inside the shed, they decided to find a place to hide just in case he looked inside. There was boxes, rakes, hoes, ropes, and equipment used in some of the activities. Surely, they could find a place where he wouldn't think to look.

"He knows this place, so he may check in here. Do you see a good place to hide, Charmaine?" Kiki asked her quietly.

"How about behind the boxes that over close to the corner?" Charmaine said as her eyes were searching the small room.

"I'm afraid that might be the first place he would look, because in the movies, they always get behind some boxes," explained Kiki. "Let's see how creative we can be."

They found a small closet in another corner of the tiny building and opened it to see what they could find. They found raincoats and some cowboy hats. Kiki had the idea of putting a coat and hat on, and then make their way to their bunkhouse to see if the others were there. Charmaine gave Kiki a big smile and told her she thought it was a good idea.

They looked for the right sizes, and Kiki decided to get the largest one for Charmaine, so it might hide her baby that was just sitting in there waiting to come out in the world. After finding their outfits, they gradually opened the squeaky door. Kiki stuck her head out first and told Charmaine it was okay to go out.

They walked toward where the bunkhouses were located. When they got to the bunkhouse where Kiki and her cousins were staying, they walked inside hoping to find her cousins, but it was empty. Kiki was disappointed, but she realized they needed to use the restroom and get a bottle of water. Kiki thought leaving something here to let the girls know that she had been here was a good idea. She drew a picture of a cabin and put her scarf on top of it and left it on her bed.

Charmaine looked at Kiki's picture and asked, "Why did you draw the cabin instead of writing a note to them?"

"I thought if the crazy man came in here, all he would see is the scarf and wouldn't even move it. If he saw a note, he would take it with him. We know if we get captured again by him, the cabin is where he will be taking us," answered Kiki with a smile. "The girls will pick up my scarf, and when they do, they will see the picture of the cabin. Charmaine, they are smart and won't have any trouble figuring it all out."

"Okay, but we need to get out of here, because you know this will be one of the first places he may look," said Charmaine, and she was probably right in her assumption.

"Alright, I say we go look around for people we know in a super quiet manner. Put on your lovely raincoat and cowboy hat. Yeehaw, let's go, girl."

CHAPTER FIFTY-THREE

After eating their hard biscuit with no flavor at all, they were led to the place behind a huge rock where they were instructed to build the shed. Stone looked around and saw a pile of lumber, hammers, and nails. There was a pile of used rusty tin roofing beside the lumber.

Stone asked the oldest with the biggest gun, "Do you have some kind of plan or blueprint of how you want this shed built?" The gun-toting men just looked at each other wondering what he was talking about.

"I guess not. Just build one, or we will have to shoot you fellers," said the shortest one, who didn't even have a gun with him.

"How big do you want it, like an eight foot by ten foot or what?" asked a smiling Beau who didn't have a clue how to begin building a shed.

Stone asked them again, "What are you going to use this shed for?"

"Oh, we going to put the moonshine still in there, so it won't smell up the barn and make the cows drunk," answered the mama who had just walked up. "Make it around twelve by twelve. That might do it. Now, get to work."

"Yes, ma'am," said a smiling Stone. He was still thinking about their drunk cows.

The cousins kept building for what seemed like all day. Stone had been thinking ever since they began building. They needed a fool-proof plan. He just had to get it all straight in his head.

"It's sort of hot out here. Could we take a break and maybe have a bottle of water, so we don't get to feeling faint? We wouldn't be any good to you if we did."

Boss Brother answered for the family, "I guess you can take a break, but it will only be for fifteen minutes."

"That's okay. Thanks," said a happy Beau.

The cousins sat together on the hard ground talking softly while waiting for their water. Stone told them they needed to get out of here, "We need a plan. They will go inside and get us some dinner in a bit, and they most likely will leave at least one of them behind with their gun. Surely there are enough of us to take down one man. I'll give you the sign when to begin. Even if they leave two of the men, we should be okay."

They all agreed to Stone's plan. It was worth a try and hoped it worked. They shouldn't have a problem with taking down a man or two. They decided not to take their guns, just get the man down. Hopefully, this would work. They could throw the gun as far as they could out in the wooded area.

CHAPTER FIFTY-FOUR

The ranch hand thought for sure they would have been in the supply shed behind the barn. There weren't many places in there to hide anyway. They may be smarter than he imagined if they could elude him in such an outdoor place. He didn't see them anywhere in the barn either. Going to the bunkhouse was a bust also. All he saw in there was girly stuff laying around. Maybe he would see them on his way to the dining area.

He sees several people sitting at the tables in the dining area. There was one table that had two ladies sitting with their backs to him, but there were two couples of older people sitting with them. Something was peculiar about the two ladies. They both had on raincoats and cowboy hats. That's when it clicked with him. Those were the coats they keep in the supply shed in case of rain for the ranch hands to use. That must be them.

The crestfallen ranch hand walked to the table and sat down beside the two women. When the women saw him, their hearts began beating overtime. The couples were happy to see that one of the ranch hands wanted to sit with them.

The sweet lady with the beautiful silver hair looked at the ranch hand, "It's so nice of you to sit with us. All of you ranch hands have been so good to us, and we appreciate it more than you can imaging. What's your name, Sonny?"

The ranch hand thought for a few seconds before answering, "My name is Joshua, ma'am. I'm here to show my sisters around the ranch," Kiki and Charmaine knew there was not a ranch hand named Joshua, so they still don't know his real name.

"That's so sweet of you. I bet you're a good brother," said the other elderly woman with the blue hair at the large table.

Charmaine and Kiki wanted to say something, but they were afraid he would do something foolish and maybe hurt one of these precious senior citizens at this table, so they kept quiet. They were in serious trouble, and they knew it. They were hoping it would end well.

When they finished eating, the ranch hand tipped his hat to the two couples that had sat with them and said, "It's been good eating with you lovely people, and I would love to stay and chat, but I better get my sisters and show them around before I finish my job for the night."

He helped Charmaine up from the table and directed her and Kiki in the direction he wanted them to go. "Where are you taking us?" asked Kiki with a little bit of fear in her blue eyes.

"What does it matter. I have a job to do, and I can do it anywhere, so shut up," said the doleful ranch hand. The ladies were worried about the job he thought he had to do.

"You don't have to be so grumpy. Your mama wouldn't be proud of you right now at the way you are acting," said Kiki who thought if she kept him talking, it would give them time to be rescued, or at least, keep them alive longer.

"Shut up. You don't know my parents. They were awful evil people. They were proud of nobody but themselves," This seemed to be upsetting him immensely. Kiki thought maybe there was something she could use.

"I'm sorry you didn't have a good relationship with your parents. That sounds awful. What about your twin sister? Would she be proud of what you are doing?" Kiki sure hoped this didn't make him madder, but she had to try something.

He appeared to be thinking this situation over in his mind, or at least, that is what Kiki was hoping he was doing. It could go either way, "No, my sister wouldn't like what I was doing, and I aim to stop with you two girls."

Kiki gave a big smile before saying, "So, we can go our own way. Is that what you mean?"

"I mean after I take care of you two, then I'm going to stop, so just get used to the idea."

CHAPTER FIFTY-FIVE

The downhearted cousins plus Roy, the Dude brothers, Tinker, and now Cheyenne left the rustic cabin feeling hopeless and depressed. They needed to find Kiki and Charmaine and quickly but didn't know exactly how to go about this feat. The only thing they could think of was to keep searching. They had to be somewhere nearby. Maybe they would be somewhere at the ranch and they kept missing them.

Queenie, after much thought, said, "I guess we could look around the ranch and start at the dining area. That seems to be the happening place where everybody goes at some time or another."

"Count me in," said a hopeful Gigi who was getting as weary as the others seemed to be, but they knew they couldn't give up. They would search all day and night if they needed to.

They all agreed to continue helping the cousins, which gave the cousins some hope. The more they had, the better the chance of finding them would be. They all decided to split up, so they could cover more space in less time.

"Could one of you yahoos please tell me what we are doing, and who are we looking for here at the ranch?" hollered a confused Cheyenne.

Tinker looked at Cheyenne with a smile and explained everything she wanted to know. Cheyenne agreed to help them in their search.

"Men, you, Tinker, and Cheyenne go to the dining area. You are all probably hungry anyway. Might as well eat while you're there. If there are other people, ask some questions about if they have seen Charmaine and Kiki," Queenie felt maybe now there were getting somewhere.

Gigi thought that was a good idea, "How about the rest of us check out the barn and that little shed behind the barn. They may be looking for a place to hide."

Queenie searched the eyes of the others and said, "I feel good about this. We will meet the rest of you at the dining area and go from there about what else to do. I just know we will find someone who has seen the missing ladies."

The unusual group went their separate ways hoping they would be able to find Kiki and Charmaine, or at least talk to someone who may have seen them. They felt the girls were somewhere at this ranch, and if they were, they intended to find them and protect them.

As one of the groups traveled to the big red barn where the barn dances were held, the others were almost to their destination of the dining area. They all had hope in their hearts they would find some information to the location of the missing friend and family member.

Gigi started hollering, "I see the barn up ahead. Let's look around inside. There can't be many hiding places in there. The dance floor took up almost all the space."

They all became somewhat excited to maybe finding their targets in the barn. The double doors weren't locked, so they marched inside and began searching for a place the girls could have hidden. There didn't seem to be too many places to hide, which made them a little disappointed.

Bambi started smiling as she got the attention of the others, "Listen to me. I see a loft up above the edge of the barn, and there's a ladder. I don't do ladders, but I bet Queenie could shimmy up that ladder like a jungle monkey."

Queenie did indeed climb up the ladder in record time. While she was doing that, Jade went to the ladder to go help Queenie search. All they could see were hay bales. They looked behind each stack to see if they might be hiding there, but they had no luck, and they knew they look extremely well.

Jade hollered down, "There are nowhere to be found up here.

Queenie and I are coming down, and we'll all decide on what to do next."

Trixie said, with a smile, when the loft girls came back down the ladder, "We need to go to the little shed behind the barn to see if we can find anything. They have to be somewhere, and that would be a good place to hide."

The others agreed, so off they went to the shed. They were amazed it wasn't locked but was glad it wasn't. After searching around the boxes and farm supplies, they started to walk out the door when Angel made a surprised sound.

They all looked at Angel at the same time, "What's wrong? Did you see something that might give us a clue?" asked Olivia.

"Yes, see what's on the nail that is sticking out on the wall to the left?" she was pointing to a nail that had a cloth hanging from it.

They all went to the nail, and Queenie pulled the cloth off the nail that held it, "Oh my goodness. It looks like the cloth of the blouse Kiki had on when she hurt her ankle. She would still have that on."

"It's her blouse, so that means they were hiding in here at some point, but they are not here now," said Olivia.

It gave them hope now that they knew the girls were somewhere on this ranch, but they didn't know why or where. They, for sure, wouldn't stop looking for them now. This was a very nice ranch, but it must have a million places a person could hide. They might narrow down some of the places because Charmaine may not be able get in some of them with her baby belly.

They hurried back to the dining area where the men, Tinker, and Cheyenne were sitting at the tables.

CHAPTER FIFTY-SIX

Roy along with the Dude brothers, Tinker, and their new member of the gang, Cheyenne, arrived at the dining area. There were several people sitting around the tables talking, laughing, and eating. The searching group didn't know what to do first. They were hungry, but they didn't need to lose sight of what their mission was.

B Dude squinted his eyes from the sunshine at the others and came up with an idea, "Why don't we sit among these people and conduct some conversation with them. Some of these people might have seen who we are looking for."

"Good idea you got there, B Dude," smiled Tinker. B Dude knew one thing. He knew he never wanted to make that huge lady mad at him. She was almost taller than a Georgia pine, and he felt like she could use that ball bat like a Texas Ranger.

B Dude and Little Dude went to a table and asked if they could sit a spell. To their delight, the woman, who was the only one at that table, was overjoyed to have the men sit with her.

"Sure, handsome men, you can sit with me anytime you want," said the woman with the biggest cowboy hat on the men had ever seen, along with the ugliest dress in the world. The lady, who must have been eighty if she was a day, glanced at the men who sat down at her table. She thought they must want a girl-friend, so she began what she thought of as flirting. She began blinking her eyes at them. She started off blinking them slowly making the Dude brothers extremely nervous. They had never had this happen to them. She must have thought her blinking slowly wasn't doing the trick, so she began batting them so fast, it would have knocked a bug a mile away if it took a notion to sit upon her eyelashes.

B Dude was confused. He thought she had something in her eye, "Ma'am, may I help you get whatever is in your eye out of there?" That must have been the wrong thing to say, because she knocked B Dude clean away from the table smack dab on the gravel. Thank goodness, he was a good sport about it all.

"I'm sorry, ma'am. I won't bother you anymore," stated B Dude in a half-smiling way. He had never been knocked off his seat by a little old lady before.

The old lady figured since she couldn't make any headway with the older one, she would take a try with the younger one, "How about you, sweety. Would you like to be my boyfriend?" That's when Little Dude jumped up like a jackrabbit and ran away as far as he could get from the dining area. His brother watched in amazement while laughing at his brother. He decided to let him run. He would get him later.

While all this was going on, Tinker and Cheyenne were sitting at another table with two couples of senior citizens. Tinker thought they were nice people, so she began talking to them and how they were enjoying being here at the dude ranch.

"We were wondering if you may have seen our friends. We seemed to have misplaced them and would like to find them. They are special to us. One of them is pregnant and her name is Charmaine. The other one has blonde hair and a sweet smile. You wouldn't have happened to come upon them, would you?"

The lady with the gray-blue hair said, "Yes, we have seen them. They sat with us while we all had lunch. The one who was pregnant didn't say too much, but the other one chatted on and on, but she was so nice to us, and made us laugh. Their brother came and sat between them and finally took them away to show them around the ranch. He seemed like such a sweet brother."

Cheyenne spoke, "Did you happen to notice which direction they went, ma'am?"

The other senior lady who was sitting at the table spoke up, "I believe they went in the direction of the barn." At least, that is what they thought she said. She didn't have her teeth in, so she may have heard wrong.

Roy saw some of the ranch hands eating at one of the tables, "May I sit with you find gentlemen?"

"Sure. Have a seat. What's your name? I'm Matthew and that one there is my brother, Mark. The other yahoo is John. Are you having fun while you're here at the dude ranch?" asked Matthew with the good personality.

"I am having fun. Thank you. My brother, Chad, works in the registration building. I usually hang with him when he's off work," explained Roy with a smile.

Roy needed to get down to business, "The group I'm with has lost two of their friends, and I was wondering if you may have seen them, since you boys know your way aroudn this ranch."

"It's possible we have seen them. What do they look like?" asked John who seemed concerned.

"One of the ladies is pregnant, and pretty far along, so she would be the one you spot for sure. The other one has blonde hair with a good personality. I know that probably describes a lot of the people here, except maybe the pregnant one. Her friends are concerned that something may have happened to them," explained Roy with what he was hoping was a good enough description.

"We will keep an eye out for them. We are a little shorthanded today. Luke is out today, because his sister is having a baby. Paul is sick himself, and Jake is out because his dad has a few things he needed to help him with today, but Mark, John, and I will certainly keep an eye out for your friends," stated Matthew with a smile.

Roy felt some better for having had this conversation with some of the ranch hands. He guessed that Matthew, Mark, and John were in the clear of taking the girls, but he wasn't sure about the ones who were absent today. He would meet back up with the Dudes, Tinker, and Cheyenne. They would all wait for the other group to show up and tell them what they found out.

The other group met back at the dining area around thirty

minutes later. The only thing they had was a piece of fabric that looked like Kiki's blouse. They decided to go to the registration building and ask Chad if he knew anything. They knew he would be concerned about Charmaine.

CHAPTER FIFTY-SEVEN

"You ladies don't know what you have done by running away from me. It just makes me madder when someone does that. What were you thinking?" said an aggravated ranch hand.

"We were thinking we wanted to get away from you because you are deranged. Only a deranged man would do things to people like you do. You sure don't want to be like your parents, do you? You don't have to be like them. You are better than that. Make your sister proud instead of making her feel bad." Kiki wanted to keep him talking. They needed the time for someone to rescue them and maybe prolong their life.

"Don't say I'm like my parents. They were evil," he seemed almost in tears when Kiki looked into his eyes.

"I know you're not, so stop acting like them. You are better than that. Stop this nonsense, get you a wife, and have a kid. You can raise that kid to be a better person and to do things right," explained Kiki with what she hoped was making him think along the lines of letting them loose. "As for what we were thinking, what would you do if someone captured you and wanted to kill you? I bet you would have done the same thing."

"Did you run to the cave first?" asked the man who wanted to torture them.

"What does it matter if we did or not?" asked Kiki. "You said your parents were evil. That must have been bad for you and your sister. You probably protected your sister, and it made it worse for you. That shows me you are not like your parents. There is good in you. Did they abuse you and you sister? Is that why you do these things to innocent people. I'm not your enemy. I would like to help you. You don't have to be like your parents. It doesn't help anything. Let your past be in your past, and don't dwell on it."

Kiki didn't know how he was going to react to her blabbering, but she was sure she would find out. Charmaine sat silently. She was afraid he would do something that would hurt her baby. Charmaine knew Kiki was trying to make him mad at her, so he would do the things to Kiki instead of her. If they come out of this alive, she wouldn't be able to thank Kiki enough for trying to help her.

"I would bet my last dime that you grew up in a nice cushy house with good parents who never touched you in anger and probably brothers and sisters who pampered you," said the rattled ranch hand.

"I didn't have a bad homelife if that's what you want to know. My parents took us to church to keep us on the straight and narrow. We love Jesus and try our best to live for him. We need to remember that no one on this earth is perfect. Only Jesus is perfect. We all fall short at times. It's not too late for you to go to church," smiled Kiki as she was hoping for the best outcome to this whole situation.

The ranch hand sat and contemplated what Kiki had just told him. Maybe she was making sense. Maybe not. He was afraid the church would fall down on the ground if he went in there, but if what Kiki was telling him, he would be welcomed in church.

"It's not too late, you can make your life better and be happier. Don't you want to be happy instead of dwelling on the past. There are a lot of people who have things in their past they would like to forget. You may not forget it, but you can put it in the back of your mind and not dwell on it," explained Kiki.

"Get up, ladies. We are going down in the hole. You'll do what I say, or I will shoot the pregnant lady."

CHAPTER FIFTY-EIGHT

After a discussion of what to do with the information they had gathered, they decided to travel to the registration building to talk to Chad about his thoughts about it all, and what he might suggest.

They made it without incident to the registration building where Chad was working. They noticed he had some customers, so they sat in the lobby waiting for Chad to be free. They were going to discuss things while waiting on Chad, but the customers were so bright he was talking to, they decided to watch. The man and woman at the desk were adorned with western clothes that had rhinestones all over them. The rhinestones were even all over their boots and their hat. When they were finished, they turned around to go outside, and that's when the man gave a huge smile showing the shining rhinestone on one of his front teeth.

"Well, that was a treat," said a happy Bambi as she watched them walk away. She was thinking they would scare their poor horses to death with all the bling. They would get thrown for sure.

"Chad, have you seen Charmaine's husband around? I wondered if he knew where she was," asked Trixie who was curious. She didn't want him to find her for sure.

When Trixie asked that question, Roy and Chad, both were looking around like they knew something, but didn't want to say what it was.

Queenie noticed Chad and Roy and their looks of mischief and said, "Okay, boys, spit it out. We won't tell anyone. Sam is not our favorite person, so why would we say anything?"

They all walked over to a corner where no one would hear their conversation. Chad and Roy were tired of keeping this all to themselves and would be glad to share it.

"First of all, Sam is Roy and my cousin. We certainly don't like what he does to Charmaine. I can't believe he's even our cousin. Roy and I met up with him a couple night's ago and were talking to him. He's hard to talk to sometimes. Roy got mad and hit Sam over the head with something, and it knocked him out. While he was out, we took him down to the basement. We left food and water, but as far as we know, he's still there. We thought we would let him cool off in case he sees his wife. We don't want you to hate us or think that we are mean people. We're not," explained Chad.

"Yipee," hollered B Dude as loud as he could. "It's about time someone gave him a dose of his own medicine."

Everyone was laughing and agreeing with B Dude. They promised they wouldn't tell anyone. They thought Roy and Chad did good.

"Okay, down to business. It seems that Sam has been taken care of for a while, so let's give Chad the information we know so far, and we can go from there," Gigi was happy to hear about Sam. It was about time someone locked him up so he couldn't get to Charmaine.

"Some ranch hands told us they were shorthanded today, because Paul, Jake, and Luke were out today for various reasons. We thought it had to be one of the those who called in sick or whatever their excuse was," said Roy with a smile. He was glad the others weren't mad at him and Chad, because of what they did to Sam.

The girl cousins told them all about the piece of cloth they found on a nail in the shed behind the barn, so they know they must be somewhere on the ranch.

Tinker and Cheyenne was next, "Some little old ladies said they ate with Charmaine and Kiki and that their brother came and got them and said he was going to show them around the ranch.

"Alright, Dude brothers, what do you have. You were sitting at a different table. What did you find out?" asked Jade who was ready to get down to business.

B Dude began to studder making the others wonder what in the world went on at that table. "Okay, let's just say that we got at the wrong table."

That only made the others curious, "Where is Little Dude? We haven't seen him since we all got together," asked a questioning Bambi. It seemed to her that now they had another one missing.

"I'm sure he will come back soon. He ran away from the old lady we were sitting with. She began flirting with us, and it scared Little Dude," said brother B Dude who started to laugh, and the other couldn't seem to control their laughter either.

"I've got an idea. We need to go back to the bunkhouse. I have a feeling I can't let go of. Something in my mind is telling me to go to the bunkhouse," said Olivia who got these feelings quite often.

CHAPTER FIFTY-NINE

The exhausted searchers all walked back to the ladies' bunkhouse hoping that the missing girls would be there waiting for them. It was a long shot, but worth trying. It seemed to be the best idea they had. They were having to make so many plans, they were running out of ideas. The cousins decided when they got home, they didn't want to even think of having to make a plan to find someone who may be in danger.

Before doing anything, they retrieved a bottle of water and a snack from the small cooler to give them energy, then they would be ready to go do whatever they needed to do. All the group was inside the bunkhouse, as they began looking around to see if there was anything unusual. They knew the girls weren't there, because they would have already made themselves available to them.

Queenie had a confused look on her face as her eyes searched around the large room with all the eight beds that had been recently made up by the maids, "Something is off in here. The maids have made the beds but look at the imprints on a couple of the beds looking like someone had been sitting on them. We haven't been in here since we left this morning. The maids wouldn't have left those wrinkles on the fresh bedspreads. Someone was in here after the maids left, and I see snack wrappers and a couple empty water bottles."

Gigi began looking around and said, "Look. That is the scarf Kiki had on when she went missing." Gigi walked over there and picked it up. Hidden under the scarf was a note left for them.

"What does it say?" asked an excited Trixie. She thought now they may have a big clue to find them. Trixie is strong, plus her captors didn't have much of a brain and never intended to kill her.

Gigi had sadness in her eyes as she told what the note said, "It basically was telling us that someone has definitely taken them and if we can't find them, to go look under the floor of the cabin."

"But we were there not too long ago," cried Angel who couldn't believe this was all happening to them. It brought back memories of last year when two men took Trixie.

"Maybe someone took them, and they escaped and came here to the bunkhouse looking for us. We have been missing them. Kiki must have known if they were caught that they would be taken to the cabin," Jade thought she was on to something.

"Get your weapons ready, ladies. Looks like we are going back to the cabin and get the girls before something bad happens to them. We can't wait much longer," Queenie was in battle mode, and she would use all her energy to get Kiki and Charmaine back.

Trixie smiled, "I'll go get my shovel." The other ladies laughed at that. It didn't take her long to retrieve her tiny shovel.

"Don't worry, ladies. I have my pistol in my pocket. Little Dude and I never go anywhere without them," said Big Dude with a smile. He was glad Trixie had a shovel until he saw it, and then he began laughing. Now he knew why the other ladies laughed when she said she would get her shovel.

As they all walked toward the door of the bunkhouse, Olivia hollered, "Stop." Everyone looked at Olivia with interest of what she had on her mind.

"What's wrong, Olivia?" asked Bambi.

"I am going to take some bandages, peroxide, and ointment with me just in case one of the girls have any injuries," explained Olivia, who wanted to be prepared.

"Good idea," said Roy. He hoped they didn't need them, but it was best to be prepared than not.

Before getting to the door, they heard a noise outside. When they looked out, they saw one of the ranch hands put something through the door handles, so they couldn't get outside. They were locked in, and the ranch hand was running away.

They noticed the windows were the small ones up nearly to the ceiling. They didn't look like they could be opened either.

"Well, look for something to break the window, and someone can go out and take whatever he had blocked the doors with, and then let the others out," said Tinker who was smiling way too big.

"Ladies and gentlemen, you forget what I carry around with me all the time," That's when they all looked at Tinker's favorite weapon, her ball bat.

CHAPTER SIXTY

The ranch hand headed back to the cabin where he left the crazy girls. He would do this last job and be done with all the hassle of trying to find people to torture like his dad did to his sister and him. Maybe the one called Kiki was on to something when she told him to go to church and be a better person, and then he would be happier. He had to admit he had never been happy, because his parents never did anything to make him and his twin sister have a happy life.

He was glad he tied them up before he went back to their bunkhouse to see if the ladies the girls came with were back there and making sure they didn't have guns or any other weapons. He didn't see any, so he could get started with the torture of the clueless girls.

"Okay, little girls. It's time to go downstairs and see my special room," said the smiling ranch hand.

He pushed toward the door that went down to that special room. He didn't see Kiki when she dropped one of her earrings on the floor at the doorway that opened to the stairs going down. After she dropped it, he pushed her almost making her fall all the way down the steps.

They were downstairs in a dimly lit room if it could even be called a room. He managed to keep his gun in his hand while putting the girls' wrists and ankles in the cuffs at the end of the chains. He really didn't want to do this, but he was committed now. He just wished Kiki hadn't made him feel bad about his actions. The more he thought about it, the more it made me wonder if she could be right. Could he really be happy?

After he got the chains on the ladies, Kiki started to speak, "Dear

Lord, we pray you will protect us, and guide us on what to do next. We want to pray that you will forgive this man of his sins and knock the evil right out of his body. We would like to see him have a happy life."

"What in the world are you doing, lady. The Lord doesn't want to help me. What would make you think He would," he was getting agitated with all that was going on in his special room.

"Because He loves everybody, even you, and He would like to see you living a better life than you're living right now. You would be much happier. Wouldn't you like to be happy?"

"Shut up." He went to the corner where he had some sort of toolbox and came back with an evil-looking tool that appeared to be able to cut off body parts.

Kiki knew they weren't going to come out of this place without some injuries or dead. She began to sweat but would not let him know he was causing pain to her. He walked by Charmaine, who had tears running down her cheeks, to where Kiki was sitting on the hard-packed dirt floor.

He put the instrument beside Kiki while he lit a cigarette. She didn't know what he intended to do to with the cigarette, but she had an idea that wasn't too good in her mind as she watched him light it up. Kiki was not going to give him the satisfaction of seeing her in pain. Maybe he would stop if she showed no pain. It might not be the best plan she ever had, but it was all she had since she was sitting in the dirt in chains.

He proceeded to put cigarette burns up and down her arm and one on each cheek, while Kiki didn't make a sound at all while he was burning her. He was confused about why she didn't make a sound. He knew from experience that it hurt.

"What's wrong with you that you aren't screaming? Are you made out of iron?" asked the ranch man who was in shock. I'll show you some pain. He picked up the cutting tool and looked Kiki in the eyes. "Let's see what you are really made of."

He started to cut off one of her fingers, but he changed his mind and just broke it instead, and that's when Kiki still didn't make a sound, but she passed out cold from the pain.

CHAPTER SIXTY-ONE

"What do we do now? Those windows are too high to jump out of, and on top of that, they look very thick," said Bambi. "I don't do jumping."

"You don't have to jump. One or two of us can jump out and then unbar the door to let the rest of you out," explained Queenie to the women who were about to panic. "Surely there is a back door. I think the fire code would make them have a back door."

"You're right. I'll check," Jade ran to the back of the large room and the bathroom to see if there was another door. "I saw a door in the back, but it was locked or bolted shut one. The bathroom has a window, but it's like these in here."

"Okay, Tinker, stand on the bed and knock the devil out of that window," said Trixie who was wanting to see her do that. She would have helped her with her shovel, but she wasn't sure if she would be any help or not.

"You got it," said a smiling Tinker. She was tall enough that she didn't have to go up too high to get to the window. "This sure is a small window, ladies. I know I'm way too big to get through it."

"That's okay. We can stick Trixie through it. She's the smallest of us," said Bambi.

"I sure hope there is a mattress out there on the ground. That's a high jump," Trixie was hesitating about going out the high window.

"Don't worry. We'll bring your shovel out when we come," laughed Olive. That's when Tinker pick her up and shoved Trixie out the window. They all heard the thump when Trixie landed on the hard ground.

"I'm okay," she hollered loud enough to be heard from the registration building. "Don't worry about me."

"Just go to the door and let us out, crazy lady," yelled Bambi who seemed to be losing her patience.

All got out as planned and the calvary began their hike to the old cabin to rescue their friend and cousin. Every one of them were determined to do their job well. There was no room for mistakes. They didn't know what they might see when they got there but was hoping for the best that Kiki and Charmaine will be alive and well.

They slowly walked up the small hill to the cabin looking like the Avengers. They stopped right before going inside. B Dude whispered, "Let's all stop and check our weapons before going inside. Then we can make a plan for entering the cabin." The ones with guns checked to make sure they were loaded. Tinker held up her ball bat while Trixie held up her four-inch shovel. The others were carrying big sticks which they held up for all to see.

Various feelings were floating around in the heads of each member of the rescue group. They knew this had to go off without a hitch.

CHAPTER SIXTY-TWO

While the group of rescuers were contemplating their entry plan, the male cousins were almost ready to put their plan in place to escape away from the men who took them and made them build their shed for their moonshine. They had to admit this was an adventure they had never had before and would probably never have it again. At least, that was what they were hoping.

Stone was right because two of them went to get their meal for the evening. Thank goodness, the one they left behind to guard the workers was not the smartest of the bunch. He looked at the others and nodded toward the one lone man who had been left behind. They understood what he was trying to tell them, and they were more than ready.

Stone looked at the man with the rifle and said, "Could you help me push in this board? I'm having some trouble with it." Stone was hoping it would work, and he was not disappointed.

"Sure," gun man said as he propped his riffle against the big rock. He walked to where Stone was standing.

Stone gave his cousins the signal they had agreed upon earlier in the day, and that's when the action began. Stone went behind the man and put his hand over the man's mouth to muffle out the noise he would most likely make. Beau held his hands behind his back while Bragg got his gun and threw it as far as he could throw. The man was trying to kick them, so Lee put his arms around the precious brother's knees.

It was working. They threw the man on the ground, who was still stunned about what had happened to him. He didn't really know what to do now. His brothers would probably give him a good lickin' for letting these men go, but to be honest, they had him outnumbered.

"Go boys, run as fast as you can to the left of here. I'm almost sure that's the way to the highway," said Stone.

"He's right. Go to the left to get to the highway," said the man without a gun as he raised his head. After telling them the way to the highway, his head fell back down in the dirt.

"Thanks," said Lee as they began to run.

They made it to the highway in record time and began walking toward the area where the truck stop was located. They couldn't wait to get back to something normal, because this definitely wasn't normal.

They found Stone's truck right where they left it and slowly walked with big smiles on their faces toward their mode of transportation to the Dude Ranch. They couldn't wait to tell the females of the group about their adventure.

"I suggest we get something to eat on the way and arrive there to see what all the girls have been doing," suggested Forrest, who was more than ready to get to the Dude Ranch, although he didn't think he wanted to get on another horse.

It was time for the shed builders to have some fun with the girls before having to travel back home.

CHAPTER SIXTY-THREE

The rescuers were standing outside the rustic cabin where they were sure held Kiki and Charmaine. They couldn't wait to get in there and get them out if they are in there, but they needed one more plan.

"The first thing we need to do is call the police department and tell them where we are and get them to meet us here. While they are on their way, we go in there and get the girls before he does something bad to them that can't be fixed," said a helpful Roy.

"You're right, Roy," said B Dude. "I will go inside first because I have a gun. Roy and Tinker can go after me, and then the rest of you come after us and wait in the living room being completely quiet."

"We all can't go downstairs, so I suggest we elect B Dude, Roy, Tinker go along with Jade, Gigi, and Olivia. The rest can wait in living room and be a look out for the police and tell what is going on," said Queenie with concern. "If anyone I mention going down doesn't want to, tell me now and I will take your place."

No one said they wouldn't go, so they walked to the door that went down to the hole and noticed something shinny on the floor going down. Roy picked it up and showed it to the others.

"That's Kiki's earring. She is leaving us clues. Oh my, let's get on down there," said Olivia who was ready to do whatever needed doing. She was praying it wasn't bad.

"Remember to walk as quietly down the stairs as you can," said B Dude as he crept down first pointing out steps that weren't there and others that squeaked.

B Dude, Roy, and Tinker were ready for battle as they slowly opened the door just a small crack so they could see inside the small room. What they saw was Charmaine chained at the wrists and ankles. When they looked closer, they saw Kiki who appeared to be passed out.

B Dude went in first with his gun aimed toward a man trying to hide in a corner, "Come out of that corner, man, and face the music. We have you now." That's when the man shot at them, thankfully, missing all of them. They thanked the Lord that the man couldn't shoot straight.

It just so happened that B Dude was an excellent shot and could hit anyone anywhere he wanted to. He shot at the ranch hand and hit him in the leg and the other shot went to his hand that was holding the gun. Tinker got in on the action when she walked to the man and hit him in his good knee with her ball bat.

While they were taking care of the ranch hand, Jade, Gigi, and Olivia were trying to free Charmaine and see if Kiki was still alive. Charmaine was crying so hard they couldn't understand half of what she was saying.

"It's okay, Charmaine. We are getting you two out of here and will take the man to the police," said Gigi as she put her arms around Charmaine shoulders to sooth her.

The rescue bunch came up the stairs with Charmaine while Jade and Olivia came up carrying an unconscious Kiki. The ones that were left in the living room just about came undone as they gazed upon their cousin who wasn't moving at all.

"Don't worry. She just passed out. It was, most likely, from the pain. He burned her with a cigarette all up and down her arms and on her cheek. Her ring finger on her left hand has been broken, but she's alive and will be fine when we get her taken care of. Thank goodness, we brought some supplies with us," explained Olivia as she looked at Kiki with tears in her eyes. The others knew Olivia would take good care of Kiki, so they would try not to worry too much.

After Roy and B Dude dragged the ranch hand out the door, they threw him on the ground. He sure wasn't going to run away. The noticed a police car getting closer to the cabin.

At the sight of the police car, the ranch hand got up the best he could and was going to try to get away. Not a smart move on his part. First of all, he couldn't run too well with a gunshot in one leg and a broken knee on the other leg. Tinker did a good job with that one.

Tinker saw the man get up and trying to walk. She must not have liked that, because she ambled over to him and hit him on the head with her ball bat. He was out like a light.

Two policemen got out of their car and walked over to Tinker. "Tinker, haven't we told you about using that ball bat on humans?"

Tinker smiled, "I'm not sure he was a human. He's the one who killed people and tortured them. Over there are the two women he had down under the cabin. One of them is with child and the other one has been burned and a finger broken. Most likely, he was going to kill them too," explained Tinker. She didn't care what they did to her. She would do it the same way all over again if she had to.

"Alright, Tinker. We didn't see anything this time but watch from now on what and who you hit with your ball bat."

"Thanks, Brandon," said Tinker as she watched the policeman go over to see what was going on.

Olivia was working on Kiki who was coming into the world again. She was still in pain, but Olivia was going to take care of her so the burns wouldn't get infected.

One of the policemen walked over to the ranch hand and looked him over. He shook his head like he couldn't believe what had been going on here at the cabin.

"Brandon, did you see what these people did to me?" said the ranch hand in a lot of pain.

"Looks like to me, Jake, you got what you deserved," smiled the policeman named Brandon.

The happy group rambled slowly back toward their bunkhouse, so Charmaine and Kiki could get some rest. There would be time later to discuss what had happened. It turned out okay, but it could have been worse, if they hadn't gotten there when they did.

When they got back to the bunkhouse, they saw the male

cousins sitting outside on the porch looking like they didn't have a care in the world. The girls were glad to see them. They took B Dude, Roy, Tinker, Charmaine, and Cheyenne over to meet the male cousin to meet their new friends, and they all promised to go eat supper together and go the barn dance afterward. What a way to end a vacation.

EPILOGUE

It was almost time for the nice ladies to get back on their bus to travel to the airport, so they can go back to their real lives as wives, mothers, and grandmothers. They love meeting each other once a year and having the fun they know they will have.

It was hard to say goodbye to all they had met while on the Dude Ranch, especially Charmaine. She became special to the ladies and they made her promised to let them know if they can help her in any way.

Chad told them before they left that Jake was taken away with all the other stunned ranch hands watching. They never would have guessed it was him that killed that woman and took Kiki and Charmaine. Jake's life was about to be completely different from now on.

As for Sam, he was let out of the basement by Chad and Roy on certain conditions. Of course, they left the door locked while giving him these conditions. Chad and Roy were not stupid. His conditions were: (1) He had to let Charmaine go home to her parents. (2) He will not bother her at all. (3) She will have divorce papers drawn up and you will sign them without hesitation. (4) You need to go to counseling.

They opened the door carefully, not knowing what Sam would do to them. Sam gave a smile that was genuine as he looked at his cousins. "I've been doing a lot of thinking while I was locked in the basement with little to no sunlight. You boys are right. I need to see a counselor. I realized what I was doing to Charmaine was not right, and I'll never be able to make it up to her. I'm going to change, and if you see me doing something I shouldn't, you have my permission to come take me down a notch or two." Chad and Roy agreed and walked out with Sam to his car.

B Dude finally found his brother who had run away from the old woman who wanted him for her boyfriend. He found him on the highway five miles from the Dude Ranch. B Dude put him in his car and away they went to go home thinking that they had fun and was glad they were there so he could help the women who wanted to get their friend and cousin out of the hands of a killer.

The ladies entered the airport bus that was taking them back so they could get home. The talking was about all the fun they had, even with the bad things that happened, they still had fun. Riding horses, tubing on the river, shooting, and especially the roping.

The barn dance with the line dancing was fun, and especially the dance where the skunk sputtered across the dance floor and everyone running to get out the small door, and they will never forget breakfast with a woman named Tinker Bell. Yep, they had fun, and everything ended well as they knew it would.

They would never forget their wild ride at the Dude Ranch, or the variety of new friends they made while there. Now they will get back to real living with their real names back. Alaska, Olive, Berm, Grandee, Jas, Callie, Phoenix, and Houston will look forward to meeting again next summer for another wild vacation, and the adventure they most likely will have.